The Red Badge of Courage

Stephen Crane

OXFORD
UNIVERSITY PRESS

OXFORD
UNIVERSITY PRESS

Oxford University Press is a department of the University of Oxford.
It furthers the University's objective of excellence in research, scholarship,
and education by publishing worldwide in

Oxford New York

Athens Auckland Bangkok Bogotá Buenos Aires Calcutta
Cape Town Chennai Dar es Salaam Delhi Florence Hong Kong Istanbul
Karachi Kuala Lumpur Madrid Melbourne Mexico City Mumbai
Nairobi Paris São Paulo Singapore Taipei Tokyo Toronto Warsaw

with associated companies in Berlin Ibadan

Oxford is a registered trade mark of Oxford University Press

Illustrated by Wu Siu Kau

Syllabus designer: David Foulds

Text processing and analysis by Luxfield Consultants Ltd

ISBN 0 19 585419 5

Printed in Hong Kong
Published by Oxford University Press (China) Ltd
18th Floor, Warwick House East, Taikoo Place, 979 King's Road, Quarry Bay
Hong Kong

THE RED BADGE OF COURAGE

The *Oxford Progressive English Readers* series provides a wide range of reading for learners of English.

Each book in the series has been written to follow the strict guidelines of a syllabus, wordlist and structure list. The texts are graded according to these guidelines; Grade 1 at a 1,400 word level, Grade 2 at a 2,100 word level, Grade 3 at a 3,100 word level, Grade 4 at a 3,700 word level and Grade 5 at a 5,000 word level.

The latest methods of text analysis, using specially designed software, ensure that readability is carefully controlled at every level. Any new words which are vital to the mood and style of the story are explained within the text, and reoccur throughout for maximum reinforcement. New language items are also clarified by attractive illustrations.

Each book has a short section containing carefully graded exercises and controlled activities, which test both global and specific understanding

CONTENTS

1

THE REGIMENT

Waiting

At last, winter left the earth. The fog rolled away, and all the army was seen stretched out on the hills, resting. As the spring sun changed the grass from brown to green, the army woke from its winter sleep. It began to tremble with eagerness as stories flew around. The soldiers watched the roads. All through the winter these roads had been like muddy streams; now they were dry enough to use again.

At the foot of the camp there was a river. Across it, at night, the men could see the fires of the enemy camp among the distant hills.

'We're going to move tomorrow!' a tall soldier told his companions. 'We're going to go up the river, cross it, and come back behind the enemy.'

He described the whole plan to them. When he had finished talking, the men in their dark blue uniforms began to argue.

'It's a lie!' said one soldier loudly. He jumped to his feet. His smooth face was red with anger. 'I don't believe this stupid old army will ever move. We've got ready to move eight times in the last two weeks, and we still haven't moved!'

The tall soldier felt that he must defend his story. He and the loud one nearly had a fight about it.

Another soldier began to curse. 'I just made a wood floor for my hut. Now I suppose I'll have to leave it,' he said.

A real battle at last

A young soldier listened eagerly to all of this. Then he went into his hut. He had a lot to think about, and he wanted to be alone.

5 So we are all going to fight at last, he thought to himself. Tomorrow, perhaps, there will be a battle. And I shall be in it.

He could hardly believe it. All his life he had dreamed of battles. In his imagination, he had taken part in them,
10 and saved many people through his courage. But when he was awake, he did not really believe in battles. They were something that happened in history.

From his home, he had heard about what was happening, but he didn't really believe there could be
15 a war in his own country. It couldn't be a real war; they didn't have those any more. Men were kinder now, or less brave, or better educated.

All the same, he had tried several times to join the army. Stories of great fighting shook the land. Perhaps
20 these battles were not quite like the ones in history books, but he longed to see the fighting for himself. His busy imagination drew it all for him in bright, fierce colours.

Henry's decision

25 His mother did not encourage him. She knew hundreds of good reasons why her son was far more important on the farm than on the field of battle. His mother was usually right.

At last, however, he decided to join. The stories in
30 the newspapers, the talk in the village, and his own imagination were stronger than his mother's arguments. There was fighting and glory, and he wanted his share.

'Ma,' he said one night. 'I'm going to join the army in the morning.'

'Don't be a fool, Henry,' said his mother. Then she turned her face to the wall and said no more.

The next morning, Henry went to the nearest town and joined the army. When he came home, his mother was milking the brown cow. 'Ma, I've done it,' he said. There was a short silence. 'I'll pray for you, Henry,' she said at last, and went on milking the cow.

A mother's tears

Later, he stood in the doorway with his uniform on his back and the light of excitement in his eyes. Then he saw two tears on his mother's thin cheeks. Still, she said no words of praise or blame. He was disappointed. He had planned comforting words and a loving goodbye. But what she said next destroyed all his plans.

'You be careful, Henry,' she said. 'Don't think you can beat the whole rebel army by yourself, you can't. You're just one small person among a lot of others, and you'll have to keep quiet and do as they tell you.

'Henry, I've made you eight pairs of socks. And I've packed all your best shirts. I want my boy to be as warm and comfortable as anyone in the army. When you get holes in your clothes, send them straight back to me. I'll mend them.

'And always choose your company carefully, Henry. There are lots of bad men in the army. They love to lead a young lad into bad ways and teach him to drink and use bad language. Don't go near them, Henry. And never do anything that you'd be ashamed to tell me about. Always behave just as you behave in front of me, and I guess you'll be all right.

'There's one more thing, Henry. Do your duty, son, and don't think about me. If a time comes when you have to choose between death and doing something shameful, Henry, don't hesitate. You just do the right thing, and don't think about me. God will take care of us all. Don't forget about the socks and the shirts, child. I've packed a home-made cake for you, too. Goodbye, Henry. Be a good boy.'

He was in a hurry to go, and this was not at all what he had expected a mother to say to her brave young son. Still, when he looked back from the gate, he saw his mother at the doorway, her face wet with tears and her thin body trembling. Then he bowed his head and felt suddenly ashamed of himself.

Afraid of running away

From his home, he walked to his old school to say goodbye. The admiring looks of the girls made him feel better. And on the way to Washington with the other soldiers, Henry's excitement grew. At every station, the people shouted and cheered. The soldiers were greeted like heroes with food and coffee and warm smiles, and he felt braver every minute

After a long journey with many stops, Henry spent many months of boring life in a camp. The army did little except try to keep warm. Perhaps I was right after all, thought Henry. There are no more real battles.

The only enemy soldiers he ever saw were some guards along the river bank. They did not do much shooting. Old soldiers told him terrible stories about the rebels, but Henry did not believe them. The old soldiers loved to frighten the younger ones, and laugh at them. *5*

However, Henry now realized that it did not much matter what the old soldiers said. Everyone agreed that the rebel soldiers were good fighters. Here was Henry's big problem. He lay on his bed thinking about it. He was trying to prove to himself that he would not run *10* away.

He had never worried about that before. He had never doubted his own courage. But now, quite suddenly, he had to admit that here was a part of himself that he did not know — it worried him a lot. *15*

This fear of running away grew in Henry's mind. As his imagination marched forward to a fight, he saw dreadful possibilities. He tried in his imagination to see himself bravely in the middle of the battle. He failed. He tried to call back his old dreams of glory, but they *20* were lost in the shadow of a real war.

He jumped up and walked about the room. 'Dear God, don't let me do anything to make Ma ashamed of me.'

Sharing his doubts

After a time, the tall soldier — the one who had been spreading the story about their move — came into the hut. The loud soldier followed. They were still arguing.

5   Henry looked at the tall soldier. 'So you think there's going to be a battle, Jim?' he said.

'Of course there is. You just wait till tomorrow. You'll see plenty of fighting.' He sounded like someone who had arranged a show for everyone to enjoy.

10   'Huh!' said the loud one from a corner.

'Well,' remarked Henry, 'I don't suppose there's much truth in the story — remember all the other stories!'

'It's true, all right,' said Jim. 'The officers have had their orders.'

15   'Rubbish!' said the loud one.

Henry was silent for a time. Then he spoke to the tall one again. 'Jim,' he said, 'do you think our regiment will fight all right?'

'Oh, I expect so,' said Jim. 'Everyone's been laughing
20   at our regiment because it's so new. There are so many young soldiers who have never fought before. But they'll fight all right, I guess.'

'Do you think any of our boys will run away?' said Henry.

25   'A few, perhaps, but there are men like that in every regiment, especially when they see their first battle. You can't be sure of anything. But I think our boys will do all right, as soon as the shooting starts.'

'What do you know about it, Jim Conklin?' shouted
30   the loud soldier. An angry argument soon followed. Meanwhile, Henry was busy with his own thoughts.

At last he interrupted them. 'Did you ever think that you might run away, Jim?' he asked, with an anxious, little laugh. The loud soldier laughed too.

'Well,' said Jim, 'if a lot of our boys ran, perhaps I'd do the same. But if everyone was standing, and fighting — I'd stand and fight too. I'm sure of that.'

'I'm not!' laughed the loud one. But Henry felt grateful for Jim's words. He had thought everyone else was quite confident and sure of themselves. He now realized that others shared his doubts, and he felt better.

True feelings

The next morning, Henry discovered that Jim's news was all a mistake. They were not moving after all. Henry was still worried, however. Now there was no chance to prove his own courage. For days he thought and wondered. At last, he decided that there was only one way to find out about himself. And that was in battle. He would have to wait for that.

Meanwhile, he tried to compare himself to his companions. Jim made him feel better. The tall soldier's calmness gave Henry confidence. He had known Jim since they were boys together. In all that time, Jim had never done anything that he, Henry, could not do too. If Jim was brave, then so was he. But then Henry thought that perhaps his friend was wrong about himself. Or perhaps Jim, who was so ordinary in peace time, would be a shining hero in war.

Henry longed to find someone else who had the fears. He tried to talk to his companions. But if anyone felt the same way, he did not show it. Henry did not dare to tell anyone his true feelings. He was afraid they would laugh, or call him a coward.

Sometimes, Henry thought they were all heroes except him. Perhaps they had secret supplies of courage that he, Henry, did not. At other times, he felt quite sure that everyone else was privately trembling and wondering, just like he was.

2

THE SUDDEN NOISE OF GUNS

Time for action

The following day, the army stayed where it was. A few days later, however, they began to prepare for action. They woke up very early. In the darkness before dawn, their uniforms glowed purple. From across the river, the fires still glittered in the rebel camp. The eastern sky was beginning to get lighter. Against it, Henry saw the huge black shape of their officer on his horse.

The regiment stood and waited. How long now, wondered Henry. He was tired of waiting. At last he heard the sound of a horse's feet. Orders, he thought. A rider stopped in front of the colonel, the chief officer of the regiment. The two held a short conversation. The soldiers struggled to hear their words.

A moment later, the regiment began to move off into the darkness. It was like a huge animal with many feet. The men marched along, arguing as they went. They still did not know what was happening.

They came to a wide road. Another dark regiment moved in front of them, and from all around, they could hear the sound of many marching men. The yellow light of day brightened behind them.

When the sun at last rose, Henry saw two long, thin, black columns of men marching ahead of him. He looked back; the columns stretched a long way behind. They were like two snakes crawling along.

Henry feels lonely

Henry could not stop thinking about his courage. He looked ahead, expecting to hear gunfire at any moment.

But the two long snakes crawled slowly from hill to hill without any loud noise or smoke. A grey cloud of dust floated away to the right. The sky above was a pure, clear blue.

Henry studied the faces of his companions for signs of any doubts like his own. He saw none. There was excitement in the air. It made Henry feel lonely and sad. Jokes were passed along the lines. The army marched to the tune of laughter.

All day they marched. When night fell, the column broke up into regiments again, and the regiments went into the fields to camp. Tents grew like strange plants. Camp fires shone like red flowers in the night.

Henry stayed quiet and alone. In the evening, he wandered away from the firelight and lay down in the grass. The moon was up, and the night was soft and still. He felt very sad and sorry for himself. He wished with all his heart that he was at home again, on the farm. I'll never be a soldier, he thought. I'll never be brave and sure of myself, like the others.

He heard a movement in the grass. It was the loud soldier. 'Oh, Wilson!' called Henry. 'Is that you?'

'Hullo, Henry — what are you doing here?'

'Thinking,' replied Henry. His companion sat down and carefully lit his pipe. 'You seem sorry for yourself, lad. What's the matter?'

'Oh, nothing,' said Henry.

Wilson is confident

Wilson began to talk about the coming battle. 'We've got those rebels now!' he said. 'We'll beat them — you'll see!' His young face was bright with eagerness.

'You were complaining about this march a while ago,' said Henry.

'I don't mind marching, if there's a good fight at the end of it,' said Wilson. 'But I don't like moving about, here and there and everywhere, with nothing to show for it except sore feet.'

5 'Well, Jim says we'll get plenty of fighting this time.'

'He's right, I guess. And we're going to win. We'll hammer them!' He got up and walked excitedly backwards and forwards. Henry watched him.

'You'll be a hero, I suppose!' said Henry bitterly.

10 The loud soldier blew a cloud of smoke from his pipe. 'I don't know,' he said calmly. 'I expect I'll do as well as the others. I'll try, anyway.'

'How do you know you won't run away?' asked Henry suddenly.

15 'Run?' said the loud one. 'Of course I won't run!' He laughed, and walked off.

Henry felt lonelier than ever. Did no one feel the way he did? He went slowly to his tent and lay down beside Jim. The tall soldier was already peacefully asleep.

20 Henry lay in the dark and thought of himself shaking with fear while others fought bravely for their country. As he struggled with his thoughts, he heard the calm voices of the men in the next tent playing cards. At last, tired out by his worries, Henry fell asleep.

25 **Facing the enemy**

Another night came, and more nights after that. The army marched and slept and marched again, but the enemy did not attack.

One grey dawn, however, Henry was kicked awake

30 by Jim. Suddenly he found himself running down a woodland road with a crowd of other men. His rifle and water-bottle banged against his body as he went. He could hear whispers all around him:

'What's all this about?' 'Why are we running?' 'Billy
— keep off my feet. You run like a cow!' 'What are
they in such a hurry for?' cursed Wilson beside him.

From the distance came a sudden noise of guns. As
he ran with his companions, Henry tried to think. But
he could think of only one thing: if he fell now, the
others would run over him. He did his best to stay on
his feet. He felt that the anxious crowd was carrying
him along with it.

The sun rose, and he could see the other regiments.
The time has come, thought Henry. I am going to be
tested. For a moment he felt weak with fear. He looked
round for a way out.

He saw at once that there was no way to escape. The
regiment was all round him. He was in a box. At once
he was filled with self-pity. He forgot that he had
chosen to join the army. I never wanted to be a soldier,
he thought. They made me join. And now they're
driving me to my death.

The regiment slid down a bank and splashed across
a little stream. As they climbed the hill on the
other side, again they heard the noise
of the big guns. Suddenly, Henry
felt curious. He struggled
up the bank towards the
strange, new noise.

He expected a battle
scene. There were some
little fields with woods
all around. On the grass
and among the trees,
small groups of soldiers
— skirmishers —
were running and
shooting.

A dark battle line of soldiers stood waiting in a sunny field. A flag waved. Other regiments struggled up the bank. They formed the line of battle and started marching slowly through the woods, after the running, shouting skirmishers.

Henry tried to observe everything. Sometimes, he tripped over fallen branches. What a stupid place to have a battle, he thought.

The skirmishers in front were still shooting. He could hear their shots among the trees. Once, the line passed over the body of a rebel soldier. He lay on his back staring up at the sky. There was a big hole in one of his boots. Henry looked hard at the white face. He wanted to read in the dead eyes the answer to his own question.

Henry's fears return

During the march through the fields and woods, Henry's excitement died. He had time to think. He had time to fear. There seemed to be danger in the trees. A house in the distance was full of fierce enemies. It's all a trap, Henry thought. The rebels are all around us. They'll attack at any moment.

He wanted to shout, and warn his companions. I'm the only one who realizes, he thought. I must tell the others! But the army marched calmly on. The men at either side of Henry all looked eager and interested. His words of warning died on his lips. They'll never believe me, he thought. They'll just call me a coward. He walked slowly, busy with his doubts and fears.

Presently, a young officer, a lieutenant, appeared and began to beat him with his sword. 'Hurry up, young man!' the lieutenant shouted. I hate him, thought Henry, he treats me like an animal. But he marched faster.

After a time, they stopped in the green light of a thick forest. The busy skirmishers were still shooting. Between the trees, Henry saw the smoke from their rifles. Many men in the regiment began to make tiny hills in front of themselves. They used stones, sticks — anything that might protect them from an enemy bullet. They began to argue. Some said it was braver to stand and fight. The experienced soldiers continued digging away like rabbits.

Soon the order to move came. It puzzled Henry. 'Why did they bring us here, then?' he asked Jim. The tall soldier did his best to explain, but it became clear that he did not know either.

They stopped. Everyone started building the little hills again. Then they were moved on again. They marched from place to place; no one knew where they were going, or why.

The battle

Henry was in a fever of impatience. He complained to Jim, 'I can't bear this much longer. What good does it do?'

Jim was eating some bread and meat. Henry admired him. The tall soldier accepted everything without complaining. When the order to move had come, he had left his little pile of earth and stones without a word. He said nothing, just followed orders.

In the afternoon, the regiment covered the same ground as it had covered that morning. Henry greeted the familiar wood and fields like old friends. However, when they marched into new country, his old fears returned. Again he struggled with his doubts.

Once he thought he had made up his mind that it was better to be killed at once, and end his troubles.

He saw death as a peaceful end. 'How stupid I was to worry about it!' he told himself. 'I'll go to a better place — where they'll understand me. Not like the lieutenant who hit me.'

The noise of the skirmishers grew louder. Rifle-fire mixed with far-away cheering. A battery of big guns spoke. Then the skirmishers appeared. They were running, and behind them, rifle shots rang out. Henry could see the hot, dangerous flashes of the rifles. Smoke clouds floated across the fields like ghosts. The noise grew louder, like a train.

Henry's regiment joined other regiments to form a brigade. Another brigade, that was ahead of him and on his right, went into action with a tearing roar. Then it was hidden behind a long wall of grey smoke. Henry forgot about death, and just stared. His eyes grew wide and his mouth hung open.

Suddenly, he felt a hand on his shoulder. It was Wilson. 'This is my first and last battle, old boy,' said the loud soldier. He was pale and his lips trembled. 'Something tells me I shan't live through this fight. Henry, I want you to take these things to my family …'

Tears of self-pity filled his eyes. He handed Henry a little yellow packet.

'Why, what — ?' began Henry. But Wilson gave him a sad look and turned away.

3

THE TEST OF COURAGE

Cowards

Henry's brigade stopped at the edge of a wood. The
men lay flat among the trees and pointed their rifles out
at the fields. They tried to look beyond the smoke. They
could see men running out of the smoke. Some shouted   5
information and waved as they hurried along. The men
of the new regiment watched and listened eagerly.

Now the noise in front grew to a thundering roar.
Henry and his companions froze in silence. They could
see a flag, surrounded by soldiers, waving angrily   10
among the smoke. A wild stream of men
poured across the fields. A battery of
big guns, pulled by frightened
horses, charged through
the running men.

A shot from a rebel battery screamed over the new regiment. It landed in the wood and exploded. Bullets began to whistle among the branches. The young lieutenant who had hit Henry was shot in the hand. He cursed loudly, like a man who has hit his thumb with a hammer. He held the wounded hand carefully away from his clean trousers. Another officer took out a handkerchief and bandaged his companion's wound. They argued about the best way to tie the bandage.

The battle flag in the distance waved about like a mad thing. The smoke was filled with bright flashes. Men came running out of the smoke: more and more, until Henry could see that the whole army was running away. Then the flag suddenly sank down like a dying man.

Wild shouts cut through the walls of smoke. Another crowd of men came running by Henry like wild horses. The experienced regiments on the right and left of the new one began to shout and laugh. 'Cowards! Watch them run!' Their shouts were mixed with the high song of the bullets and the thunder of the big balls from the batteries.

Fear ran quickly through the new regiment. 'My God! Saunders's men are beaten!' whispered a man beside Henry. He looked around him. The men of his own regiment were standing firm, in the middle of the crowd of running, frightened men. Here and there, officers were being carried along with the stream of soldiers like leaves in a flood. They cursed and shouted at their men, but the men still ran.

The commander of the frightened brigade rode about, shouting. His hat was gone and his clothes were torn. He shouted at his men to stand and fight, but they took no notice. They just wanted to get away as fast as possible.

Henry saw fear in the men's faces. He could not see
the thing that frightened them — not yet. The dragon
that chased them had not yet appeared. Henry feared
it, but he was curious, too. He wanted to see it. And
then, he thought, I shall probably run better than the   5
best of them!

Fire!

After a short wait, someone shouted, 'Here they come!'
The men of the new regiment checked their rifles. Jim
tied a red handkerchief round his throat. 'Here they   10
come!' came the shout again. A crowd of men charged
through the smoke. Someone near the front carried a
flag. As he caught sight of them, Henry suddenly could
not remember whether his rifle was loaded.

A general stopped his sweating horse near the   15
colonel of Henry's regiment. 'You've got to hold them
back!' he shouted fiercely.

'We'll do our best, General!' the colonel replied. He
turned to his men. 'Now, boys, save your bullets. Don't
fire until I tell you. Wait till they come close —'   20

Sweat ran down Henry's face. He wiped it away with
his coat sleeve. His mouth hung open. He got one
good, long look at the rebels before him. Then he
stopped worrying about his gun. Before he was ready
to begin — before he had decided that he was going   25
to fight — he put up his rifle and fired his first bullet.
The weapon was loaded. At once, Henry was shooting
like a machine. Load — fire — load again. He suddenly
stopped worrying about himself. He was not a man any
more. He was a member of his regiment. Something of   30
which he was a part — a regiment, an army, a country
— was in trouble. He had become a part of that larger
whole. He could not run away: can a finger run away

from the hand it belongs to? Perhaps if he thought the whole regiment was about to die, Henry could cut himself off from it. But that was not happening, so he continued working, like a small wheel in a big machine.

5 All the time he was conscious of his companions. They were brothers in battle, among the smoke and the danger of death. He was doing his job, as fast as possible. Presently, he became conscious of his own discomfort — the sweat, the burning eyes, the roaring
10 noise in his ears. After this came red anger. He became like a gentle cow that is bothered by dogs. He hated everyone. He hated his rifle because it would only take one life at a time. He longed for the power to brush the whole rebel army away with one blow. He realized
15 his own weakness, and that made him angrier than ever.

Beside him, many of his companions were cursing, shouting and praying. 'Why don't they send men to support us?' said Henry without understanding. He was
20 like a machine: fire, load and fire again …

The young soldier

This battle was not at all like the painted battles of history. No one stood up proudly like a hero. Everyone was too busy. Even the officers were rushing about
25 roaring orders and encouragement, and trying to observe the enemy on the other side of the thick smoke.

The lieutenant who had hit Henry was now beating a frightened young soldier. This lad had run, screaming, as soon as he heard the first bullet. Behind the lines of
30 fighting men, these two were acting out a little scene. The boy was crying like a child. He looked with big, frightened eyes at the lieutenant, who was shaking him like a rat.

'Get back!' shouted the officer,
and the lad went like a beaten animal.
Perhaps his fear of the officer was even stronger than
his fear of the enemy. He tried to load his rifle, but his
hands shook too much. The lieutenant had to help him.   5

Men fell here and there like bundles of old clothes.
One of the captains of Henry's brigade was killed early
in the battle. His body lay stretched out like a tired man
resting, but on the dead face was a sad, surprised look.
Farther up the line, a man was standing behind a tree.   10
A bullet had broken his knee, and he was holding on
to the tree with both arms. There he stayed, holding on
to the tree and crying for help.

Victory?

At last a shout of victory broke out along the line. The   15
noise of the guns died away, and the smoke slowly
cleared. Henry saw that the enemy was scattered. The
tide of rebels had pulled back, leaving men and
weapons, like rubbish, upon the ground.

Some men in the regiment began to cheer. Many were silent. The fever left Henry's blood, and he suddenly realized how thick and smoky the air was. He was dirty and sweating. He took a long drink from his
5 water-bottle.

The news traveled quickly up and down the line. 'Well, we've held them back.' Henry turned to look around him. It was good to have time to look. Beneath their feet, a few bodies lay still. They lay in twisted,
10 unnatural positions. From a position behind the wood, a battery fired. The flash of the guns frightened Henry at first. He thought they were aiming at him.

A small group of wounded men moved slowly back, like a stream of blood from the torn body of the
15 brigade. In other places, the battle continued. From a sloping hill came the sound of cheering and shooting. Smoke drifted slowly through the trees.

The thunder of the batteries was heard again. Here and there flags splashed bits of warm colour over the
20 dark lines of soldiers. Henry felt glad and excited. He listened to the noises that came from many directions. He realized then that the fighting was going on everywhere. As he looked around him, Henry felt a sudden flash of surprise at the pure, blue sky and the
25 sunlight glittering on the trees and fields. It surprised him to think that Nature was calmly going on with her business while men were doing their best to destroy each other.

Henry came slowly out of his day-dream. He wiped
30 his sweating face. So it was all over at last! He had passed the great test.

He felt a deep self-satisfaction. He had never felt so delighted with himself before. In his mind's eye, he saw himself standing firm in the heat of the battle. He felt
35 that he was a fine young man, even a hero. He gave

warm, friendly smiles to his companions. They smiled back at him. He helped a wounded friend to bandage his leg. Now we can rest, he thought.

The enemy again

Suddenly a shout broke out along the lines of the new regiment. 'Here they come again! Here they come again!' Henry stared. Surely not, he thought, this is impossible. This can't be happening. We beat them! It's all a mistake.

But the shooting began, and with it came the smoke. The smoke clouds were a dirty yellow in the sunlight and a sad blue in the shadow. The flag was sometimes hidden in the smoke, but usually it shone above it, glittering in the sun.

A dull, tired look came into Henry's eyes. His whole body trembled with tiredness. All the strength had left his arms. His hands felt big and useless, as if he wore gloves. His knees felt very weak.

How brave and strong the enemy must be, he thought. They don't think this is too much of a good thing! I'm so tired, I can hardly stand. But here they come — they must be made of steel. Machines, that's what they are. Machines. Put a little oil in, wind them up, and they'll fight until sunset.

He slowly lifted his rifle and fired at a group of rebels. One fell, the rest continued to charge. A man near Henry had been shooting hard; now, quickly he dropped his gun and ran away screaming. Another lad suddenly grew pale and ran. There was no shame in his face. He ran like a rabbit. Others began to run away through the smoke. Henry turned his head to look. It seemed as if his whole regiment was breaking up and running away.

BETWEEN LIFE AND DEATH

Run for your life!

With a cry of fear, Henry turned round. For a moment, in the noise and the smoke, he lost his sense of direction. Danger threatened him from every side. He began to run away from the charging rebels. His rifle was gone. His water-bottle banged against his side as he ran. His face was grey with fear.

The young lieutenant jumped forward with a shout. Henry saw his angry red face. The lieutenant lifted his sword. Fool! thought Henry. Why doesn't he run too? He ran and ran, staggering like a blind man. Two or three times he fell down. Once he tripped over a branch and fell flat on his face.

Since he had turned his back on the fight, his fears had grown and grown. Death that threatened him from behind was far more terrible than death staring him in the face. The noises of the battle rang in his ears. They seemed to be coming closer. He ran and ran. Before him and behind him and on either side of him, other men ran too. In a strange way this comforted Henry. Surely the dragon that was chasing them would eat the nearest ones first. So Henry ran faster, to put as many people as possible between himself and the dragon.

He led the wild race across a little field. Shots exploded all around. They came from the batteries, and they flew through the air with long, wild screams. Once one fell in front of him and exploded with a bang and a flash. He fell flat on the ground. Then he jumped up 5 and staggered away through some bushes.

The general

He saw a gun battery in action. The men there did not seem to know anything about the terrible battle that was going on a few hundred yards away. The battery 10 was having a private argument with a distant enemy. Its gunners were busily loading their guns and admiring their own shooting. They stroked their big guns and encouraged them all the time. They treat them like horses, Henry thought.

He saw a brigade going to support another. He watched it marching smoothly along, with its weapons shining and its bright flags flying. Officers were shouting. This sight also filled him with wonder. The brigade was hurrying into the mouth of death. The war dragon would eat it all up. What kind of men are they? he thought. They must all 25 be heroes — or fools, who can't understand the danger.

Henry moved on, slower now, because the noise was not so bad, and he had left the worst of the shooting behind him. He saw a general with his officers. The general sat quietly on his shining horse, looking at the
5 battle in an interested way, while his officers rushed about. Sometimes the general was surrounded by riders. At other times he was quite alone. He looked busy and anxious. He had the look of a businessman who is afraid of losing his money if he does the wrong thing.
10 Henry crept nearer. He heard the general call out, 'Tompkins, go over and see Taylor. Tell him to send help — tell him I think the centre will break up if we don't send support. Tell him to hurry up.'

A handsome, young officer on a fine, brown horse
15 rode off at top speed with the message. He left a cloud of dust behind him.

However, a moment later, Henry saw the general waving excitedly. 'Yes, by heavens, they have!' he shouted. His face burned with excitement. 'Yes, by
20 heavens, they've held them back!'

He began to roar at his officers: 'We'll hammer them now!' He shouted to a young captain, 'Here, you — Jones — ride after Tompkins — see Taylor — tell him to throw everything he's got at the enemy!'

25 ## We've won

Henry saw and heard everything. By heavens, he thought, our army won after all! In the distance, the flags waved. He could hear cheers. He stood on the tips of his toes and looked in the direction of the fight.
30 A yellow fog lay over the tops of the trees. From under it came the crack of rifle-fire. He turned away. He felt puzzled and angry. He felt that he had been badly treated.

He had run away from the charging dragon. He had been right, he felt, to save himself. After all, he thought, I am a little piece of the army. It is my duty to save myself if I can. Then the officers can put all the little pieces together again, and make another army with them. He was sure he was right. If none of the little pieces was wise enough to escape, where would the army be? He felt more and more sure that he had acted wisely and well. He might be dead if he had not run.

He thought about his companions. The blue line had stood against the enemy and won. He felt bitter about it. They had stood there because they were too stupid to run, and they had won. He felt a great anger against his companions.

What will they say, he asked himself, when I come back to camp? They'll shout at me, throw stones at me, perhaps? They are too stupid to understand. He moved slowly along with his head down. When he looked up, trembling at each sound, his eyes were the eyes of a guilty man who has no words to defend himself.

The face of death

He left the fields and walked into a thick wood. He wanted to get away from the noise of the guns that spoke to him like accusing voices. The ground was covered with bushes and plants. He had to force his way through. After a time, the noise of battle grew faint.

The sun suddenly blazed among the trees. Insects and birds sang and flew about merrily. Henry threw a stick at a small rabbit. It ran away at once. This small scene encouraged Henry. 'There!' he said to himself. 'It runs from danger — that is Nature's way. The small creature did not stand and fight the danger. It ran. Nature knows best, and I did the natural thing.'

He walked deeper and deeper into the forest. At last he reached a place where the high branches of the trees curved over his head like a church roof. It was quiet and peaceful under the green leaves.

5   Then Henry saw a terrible thing. A dead man was staring at him. He was sitting with his back against a tree. The body was dressed in a uniform that had once been blue. Now the cloth was faded to a dull green. The eyes that stared at Henry were a dull grey, like a
10   dead fish. The mouth was open. Its natural red had changed to a terrible yellow. Little ants ran over the grey skin of the face. One was busily carrying a dead leaf along the upper lip.

Henry screamed. For a long moment he stood like a
15   stone. He stared into the liquid-looking eyes. The dead man and the living man exchanged a long look. Then Henry carefully took a step backwards. He took another step. All the time he remained staring at the thing against the tree. He was afraid if he turned his back,
20   the body might jump up and chase him.

The branches pushed against him. They threatened to throw him forward, onto the body. His feet caught in the bushes and branches as he tried to escape. And all the time a soft, deep voice inside his brain whispered,
25   'Touch it! Touch it!' He trembled all over at the thought.

At last he tore himself away. He turned and ran, with the branches catching at his clothes all the way. In his mind's eye, he still saw the black ants crawling greedily over the grey face and into the dead eyes. He left the
30   little green church behind. A sad silence returned to it.

'What fools we were!'

The trees began to whisper their gentle evening prayers. The sun sank down over the hill, and insects and birds were silent.

Suddenly, the still air was torn by a distant and terrible noise. Surely, worlds were being torn apart. There were big and small guns, shouts and screams. Henry stopped. His mind 5 flew in all directions. He imagined the two armies tearing at each other's throats like mad dogs. He listened for a time. Then he began to run in the direction of the battle. He realized that it was a strange thing for him to do. He had just escaped the dragon, 10 and now he was rushing towards it. But he was curious in spite of all his fears. If the earth was about to hit the moon, there would be plenty of people wanting to watch; Henry felt like this too.

As he ran, he realized that the noises he heard were 15 part of a very big battle. He now understood that the fight in which he had taken part was, after all, quite small and unimportant. This battle was quite different. Its noise was huge and terrible and earth-shaking.

What fools we all were! Henry thought as he 20 remembered his own small fight. We took ourselves and

the enemy very seriously. We really thought we were winning the whole war. We were being heroes, we thought, doing great things that everyone would remember afterwards! When the newspapers report our
5 battle, they will see it quite differently.

Henry watches the battle

He ran and ran. He wanted to get to the edge of the forest and look out. As he ran, he imagined the battle that was going on. Sometimes the bushes tore at him.
10 Sometimes the trees stretched out their branches and tried to seize him. Perhaps, he thought, Nature does not want me to die. But he went over and through and round. At last he came to a place where he could see long grey walls of battle smoke.

15 He knew the soldiers were behind the smoke. The voice of the batteries shook him. The rifle shots cracked and flashed and hurt his ears and eyes. He stood for a moment with wide eyes and open mouth, taking in the sights and sounds. He stared as hard as he could in the
20 direction of the fight.

Then he went forward again. To him the battle was like a huge and terrible machine. He longed to watch it turning and tearing and killing, in spite of his fear.

He came to a fence and climbed over it. On the other
25 side, clothes and guns lay on the ground. A newspaper, folded up, lay in the dirt. A dead soldier was stretched out with his face hidden by one arm. Farther off there was a group of four bodies lying sadly side by side.

In this place, Henry felt like a stranger from another
30 world. This forgotten part of the battleground belonged to the dead men. He hurried away; he had a faint feeling that one of the stiff bodies was going to sit up and shout at him.

THE FALLING TREE

Wounded soldiers

Henry finally came to a road. From it he could see small groups of soldiers fighting in the distance. Smoke gathered in clouds around them. A crowd of wounded men staggered painfully along together. They were cursing and crying. Their small voices mixed with the brave roar of the batteries, the sharp cracks of the rifles and the loud cheers of the fighting men.

One of the wounded men had a shoe full of blood. He hopped about like a schoolboy in a game. He was laughing wildly. One was cursing and shouting, and blaming his officers' stupidity for his wounded arm. 'It's all their fault!' he kept repeating. Another wounded man was marching proudly, with his eyes staring straight ahead and a terrible smile on his face. As he marched, he sang a little song in a trembling voice.

Another soldier had the grey mark of death already on his face. His lips were two hard, tight lines, and his teeth were shut like a trap. His hands were covered with blood, because he had pressed them upon his wound. He moved like the ghost of a soldier, his eyes staring into the unknown.

An officer was carried along by two men. He was complaining. 'Don't shake me about like that, you fool,' he cried. 'Do you think my leg is made of iron? If you can't carry me properly, put me down and let someone else do it.' He shouted at the crowd of staggering men. 'Hey — let us pass, I say — let us pass!'

The men let the officer go past, making rude remarks about him as they did so. When he shouted and cursed in reply, and threatened them, they told him to go to the devil.

From time to time, messengers hurried through, scattering the wounded men to the right and left. Sometimes their slow, painful march was disturbed by batteries of heavy guns being pulled along quickly by teams of horses. They came along the road with a noise like thunder, their officers shouting, 'Clear the way!'

A good fight

A wounded man marched quietly at Henry's side. His uniform was torn. His skin was covered with dirt and dust and blood. Henry saw with surprise that the soldier had two wounds. One was in his head. It was tied up with a rough bandage which was covered with old black blood and new red blood. The other wound was in his arm. The wounded arm hung at his side like a broken stick.

After they had walked side by side for some time, the man spoke softly to Henry. 'That was a good fight, wasn't it?' he said.

Henry was deep in thought. He looked up into the wounded soldier's face. 'What did you say?' he asked.

'It was a good fight, wasn't it?' repeated the man.

'Yes,' said Henry. He walked faster. He wanted to get away, but the wounded man hurried painfully after him. He needed a friend to talk to.

'Yes, it was a good fight!' he began again in a small voice. 'I never saw anyone fight as well as our boys.'

He breathed a deep sigh, and looked towards Henry for encouragement. He received none, but he went on anyway. 'I was talking on guard duty with a man from the rebel army, one day. That lad said, "You and your friends will all run like rabbits as soon as you hear a gun." "Perhaps we will," I said, "but I don't think so," and I added, "and perhaps your boys will run like rabbits before we do!"'

He laughed. 'Well, our boys didn't run away today. And neither did the rebels. We all fought like tigers. Yes, sir, like tigers.'

The wounded man's kind, stupid face shone with the light of his love for the army. To him it was everything that was beautiful and strong. After a time, he turned to Henry again. 'Where are you hurt, old boy?' he asked kindly.

Henry's heart seemed to stop. 'What?' he asked.

'Where are you hurt, son?'

'Well,' said Henry, 'I, I — that is, I —' He turned suddenly and slid away through the crowd. His face was red with shame. The wounded man watched him go in surprise. Henry stood by the side of the road until his companion was out of sight. Then he started to walk with the others.

He was surrounded by wounds. There was blood and pain everywhere. Because of the question he had been asked, Henry now felt full of shame. He felt that the word 'COWARD' was written on his face in letters of fire. They all know I am not wounded, he thought. That's why they are looking at me.

Sometimes he looked at the wounded soldiers with a strange jealousy. They were hurt; they did not need to fight any more. He wished that he, too, had a wound. Then he could wear it like a red badge of courage.

Jim

Another man, walking at his side, was close to death. Henry could see from his grey, sick face that he would not live long. The man was moving stiffly and carefully. Any sudden movement would wake the pain of his wounds. As he went on and on, he seemed to be looking for something. He was like a man searching for his own grave.

Something about the man's tall figure seemed familiar to Henry. Suddenly he recognized the sick man.

'My God! Jim Conklin!'

The tall soldier gave a polite little smile. 'Hullo, Henry.'

'Oh, Jim — Oh, Jim,' he breathed.

The tall soldier held out his bloody hand. 'Where have you been, Henry?' he asked. He went on in a quiet, dull voice, 'I thought you'd been killed. So many have died today. I was worried about you.'

Henry was crying now. 'Oh, Jim — Oh, Jim —'

'You know,' said Jim, 'I was out there.' He gave a careful little wave towards the battlefield. 'What a circus it was! And, my God, I got shot. Yes, I got shot, Henry.' He repeated this fact in a surprised way.

Henry reached out his arms to help his friend. But the tall soldier went firmly on, like a machine.

Suddenly, as the two friends walked on, Jim's face froze with fear. Paler than ever, he seized Henry's arm and looked all around him like a guilty man with a secret. He spoke in a shaking whisper:

'I'll tell you something, Henry. I'm afraid. Yes, I am. I'm afraid I'll fall down, and then one of those big guns will run over me. That's what I'm afraid of —'

'I'll take care of you, Jim! I promise!'

'Will you Henry? Will you really take care of me?'

Jim hung on to Henry's arm like a baby. His eyes rolled about wildly. 'I was always a good friend to you, wasn't I, Henry? And it isn't much to ask, is it? Just pull me out of the way of the horses and the guns — I'd do it for you, wouldn't I?' He looked anxiously into his friend's face.

Henry tried to speak, but his throat was too tight. He could only nod.

'Where does he get his strength from?'

Jim suddenly seemed to forget all his fears. He began to march forward again with a face like stone. Once again, his eyes stared into the unknown. Henry wanted his friend to lean upon him, but Jim only shook his head and breathed, 'No, no — leave me alone. Leave me alone.' He moved with a mysterious purpose.

Presently, Henry heard a quiet voice beside him. He turned and saw that it was the man with two wounds again. 'You'd better take him out of the road, friend. There's a battery coming along here fast. It'll run over him. He won't live more than another few minutes anyway. You can see that. You'd better take him out of the road as fast as you can. My God, where does he get his strength from?'

'God knows!' cried Henry. He shook his hands in a helpless way. Then he ran forward and seized his friend by the arm. 'Jim, Jim!' he begged. 'Come with me.'

Weakly Jim tried to pull himself away. 'What?' he said. 'What's the matter?' He stared at Henry for a moment.

At last he seemed to understand. 'You want me to go into the fields? Oh!' He moved through the grass like a blind man.

Henry turned once to look at the fast-moving horses and guns of the battery. He had pulled Jim off the road just in time. Then a sharp cry from the other man made him turn back again.

'My God! He's running!' the man shouted.

Jim is dying

Henry saw Jim staggering towards some bushes. The sight tore at Henry's heart. He and the wounded man began to run after him. It was a strange race.

When he came closer, Henry shouted to Jim to stop. He struggled to find the words. 'Jim,' he called, 'Jim — what are you doing? You'll hurt yourself —'

The same look of purpose was in Jim's face. He was still staring into the unknown. He did not want to be disturbed. 'No, no —' he breathed. 'Don't touch me. Leave me alone —'

At last they saw him stop and stand still. They hurried towards him. The look on his face told them everything. He had at last found the place he had been searching for. His tall body stood very straight; his bleeding hands were at his sides. He seemed to be waiting patiently for something or someone. The other two watched and waited.

There was a long silence. Finally, Jim's chest began to move up and down quickly. Every breath was a struggle. It was as if an animal was in there, fighting to get out. It hurt Henry to see his friend suffering. The look in Jim's eyes was like a knife in his heart. Henry sank to the ground with tears pouring down his face. He could not bear to look. 'Jim,' he cried, 'Jim —'

'Leave me alone, Henry — don't touch me. Just leave me alone —'

There was another painful silence. Suddenly, Jim's whole body became stiff and straight. Then he shook all over. He no longer had any control over his arms   5
and legs. He trembled like a leaf in the wind, and he stared into space. His face was still, while every muscle of his body shook.

His tall body stretched itself to its full height. Then it began to swing forward, slow and straight, like a   10
falling tree. With a little cry, Jim crashed to the ground. 'God!' breathed the other man quietly.

Henry watched all of this. His face was twisted with pain for his friend. Now he jumped up and looked into the pale, dead face. The mouth was open and the teeth   15
showed in a laugh.

The blue coat fell open, and Henry saw his friend's body. The left side looked as if wolves had torn it. Henry turned and, with a sudden, wild anger, he looked towards the battlefield. 'Oh, Hell!' he cried. Then he fell onto the grass beside the body of his friend, tears running down his face.

Henry Fleming — the Coward

Not another death!

Henry was lying on the ground, close to Jim, crying. His wounded companion stood watching. 'Look here, friend,' he said after a time. 'He's dead and gone now,
5 isn't he? We should start thinking about ourselves. His troubles are all over. Nobody can hurt him now. But I must say, I'm not in the best of health myself.'

Henry looked up quickly. He saw that the man was staggering a little on his tired legs. His face had become
10 a sick, grey-blue colour.

'Good God!' Henry cried in fear, 'You aren't going to, to — ? Not you too?'

The other waved his hand. 'Oh no,' he said. 'All I want is some pea soup and a good bed.' He smiled
15 weakly.

Henry nodded.

'He was a brave lad,' said the wounded soldier again. Then they turned their backs on the body and walked away.

20 'I'm starting to feel rather ill,' said the wounded man after a little silence. He looked at Henry. 'In fact, I'm starting to feel very ill.'

'Oh, God!' said Henry. He did not think he could bear to watch another death.

25 His companion saw his fear. 'But I'm not going to die just yet!' he said. 'Too many people depend on me. I've got a wife and children at home. I mustn't die! I can't leave them!'

Henry's secret shame

As they walked slowly on, the wounded man continued
to talk.

'By the way, do you know Tom Jamison?'

Henry shook his head.   5

'Tom lives next door to me at home. He's a good lad,
and we were always good friends. Well, when we were
fighting this afternoon, suddenly Tom began to shout
at me. "You're hit, you fool!" he said to me. I put up
my hand to my head, and I saw the blood on my   10
fingers. Then before I could get away, another bullet
hit me in the arm. I got frightened then, and I ran away
as fast as I could. Just think — if Tom hadn't told me,
I might still be out there, shooting!'

There was another, long silence. Then the man said   15
quietly, 'I've got two wounds — they're only little ones,
but they're starting to trouble me now. I don't think I
can walk much further.' He looked closely at Henry.
'You look pale yourself, friend,' he said. 'I'm sure you've
got a worse wound than you realize. You should take   20
care of yourself. Where are you hurt?'

He did not wait for Henry to answer.

'I saw a man in my regiment get hit in the head once,'
he continued, 'and everyone shouted to him, "Are you
hurt, John?" "No," he said. He just looked a little   25
surprised, and he went on telling us how well he felt.
But in five minutes he was dead. So you should take
care, friend. You think you're all right, but you can't be
sure. Come on, tell me — where are you hurt? Do you
need some help?'   30

This talk of wounds made Henry feel guilty and
uncomfortable again. 'Oh, leave me alone! Just leave
me alone,' he shouted in a low, angry voice. He raised
his hand in a threatening way.

'Well, God knows I don't want to trouble anyone,' said the wounded man. 'I've got enough troubles of my own already.'

Henry looked at him with hate and fear. Suddenly, he knew what he must do. 'Goodbye,' he said in a cold, hard voice. He began to walk away. Behind him, he could still hear the man's voice calling to him. Once he turned, and saw him wandering about in the field. He looked lonely and helpless.

Henry wished he was dead. He even felt jealous of the dead men who lay peacefully among the leaves and grass.

The wounded man's simple, gentle questions had cut him like knives. The man knew nothing about him, Henry realized, but he felt that soon everyone would discover the truth. There was nothing he could do about it. Soon everyone would know his secret shame.

More deserters

The roar of the battle grew louder. As Henry walked along, he saw great, brown smoke clouds floating in front of him. The noise was coming closer. Some soldiers came out of the woods and ran across the fields.

As he came round a small hill, Henry saw that the road was full of wagons, beasts and men. He heard loud shouts, sharp orders and many curses. Fear was sweeping them all along. The drivers cracked their whips; the horses pulled and struggled. The wagons, *5* with their white cloth tops, crawled painfully along.

In some ways, Henry felt comforted by this sight. They were all moving away from the battle. Perhaps I am not so bad after all, he thought. He sat down and watched the wagons. They were like huge, slow, *10* frightened animals. The fact that their drivers were so eager to escape encouraged Henry. If the dangers of the battle frightened other men, too, then his own fear was quite natural.

Meeting the dragon   *15*

Presently, a column of soldiers came in the other direction. They were marching quickly towards the battle. The men at the head of the column hit the wagon drivers with their guns.

'Let us pass, there!' they shouted angrily. The wagon drivers hit the horses with their whips. The soldiers forced their way through.

Henry felt uncomfortable again. These men were going forward to the heart of the battle. They were going to face the enemy. They were attacking, while the rest of the army was trying to escape. The soldiers pushed the wagons to one side in their eagerness to get at the enemy. Their faces were hard and serious. Their officers' backs were very stiff and straight.

As Henry looked at them, the black weight of his sorrow fell on him again. He felt that he was watching a regiment of gods and heroes, with weapons of flame and flags of sunlight. I could never be like them, he thought. He was near to tears. How can they hurry like that? What makes them so brave? As he watched, his jealousy grew. He longed to be one of those soldiers marching into battle.

In his mind's eye, he saw himself leading the attack with a broken sword in his hand and a determined look on his face. He saw himself dying a hero's death on a hill, before the eyes of everyone. These thoughts helped him to feel braver. In his ears, he heard the shouts of victory. He felt the excitement of a fierce, successful attack. The music of the marching feet, the sharp voices of the column near him lifted him up on the red wings of war. For a few moments, he was in heaven.

He thought that he was about to set off for the battlefield, but then he hesitated. I have no rifle, he thought. Well, said the other half of Henry's mind, there are plenty of rifles around. But I shan't be able to find my own regiment, complained Henry. Well, you can fight with any regiment, can't you? the other voice said.

He started forward slowly. Then he stopped. He was struggling with his doubts. They'll see me, and they'll know I ran away, he thought. But they won't know you in the heat of the battle, the other voice told him. They won't care who you are.

But if they ask, 'Where did you come from?', what can I say? Henry asked himself. He tried hard to think of a good reply. Gradually, his courage weakened and died.

Henry hates himself

Henry was not too disappointed about all of this. It was probably wiser to stay out of trouble. Meanwhile, he realized that he was feeling very weak and ill. He had a burning thirst. His face was dry and sore and covered with dust. Every bone in his body ached. His feet were very sore, and his whole body called for food. There was a dull, heavy feeling in his stomach. When he tried to walk, he trembled and staggered with tiredness. He could no longer see very clearly. Green clouds floated before his eyes.

In all his fear and worry, he had forgotten his physical problems. Now he had to pay attention to them, and he had to admit that he felt very weak indeed. This, more than anything else, made him hate himself. I'm not like those others, he thought. I'm too soft. I'll never be a hero. I'm just a poor, weak coward.

Still, he had to know what was happening. He had a great desire to see the battle, and to get news. He wanted to know who was winning.

He told himself that, in spite of his terrible sufferings, he had never lost his greed for victory. And yet, he also told himself, he had to admit that a defeat for the army could be helpful to him. The blows of the enemy would scatter the regiments. And so, many brave men would be separated from their regiments. He would just be one of them.

A defeat would prove to everyone that he, Henry, was right to run away. That was Henry's next idea. He thought it would prove that he was wiser than the others. He had seen the danger, and done the right thing.

A good excuse for his actions seemed very important to Henry. He knew in his heart that he had behaved badly. He needed an explanation that would protect him from the hate and anger of his companions.

What next?

These thoughts rushed through Henry's mind. He tried to push them away. He hated himself for thinking only of his own future. How could he hope for defeat for his own companions? He saw them in his mind's eye, dying bravely. If he wished for that, why, he was as bad as a murderer.

Again, he thought, I wish I was dead. Everyone is sorry for the dead men; no one blames them for anything. Perhaps they were getting ready to run away when they were killed. Perhaps they died before they could pass — or fail — the test. It's just not fair!

He had thought of a defeat of the army as a way of escape for himself. He realized now, however, that it was useless to think of such a thing. Henry had been taught to believe in the strength of the blue army. This huge war machine could not fail.

Now Henry tried to think of a good excuse to take back to his regiment. He had to explain his absence, and he searched for a story. He thought of many, but he quickly saw weak places in all of them.

He imagined the whole regiment talking about him. 'Henry Fleming? Oh, he ran away!' Everywhere I go, he thought, they will look at me, and whisper, 'There goes Henry Fleming — the coward!'

A RED BADGE FOR HENRY

Like frightened animals

The column that had forced its way through the wagons was just out of sight now. Henry looked towards the woods and fields. He suddenly saw dark waves of men sweeping out of them. He knew at once that they were 5 running away. The soldiers charged towards him like frightened animals.

Behind them, blue smoke rose above the tops of the trees. Through the bushes Henry could sometimes see a distant pink glow. The voices of the batteries roared 10 like lions.

Henry was frozen with fear. He forgot his doubts and his long arguments with his conscience. We have lost the fight! he thought. The dragons are coming! The army is helpless. 15

Something inside him wanted to cry out. He had a sudden desire to make a speech to the men, or to sing a battle song. But all he could say was 'What, what — what's the matter?'

Soon they were all around him. They were leaping 20 and running, and he was in the middle of them. Their pale faces shone in the dying light. Henry turned from one man to the next as they rushed along. Some appeared to be talking wildly to themselves. No one took any notice of Henry. 25

Henry finally seized a man by the arm. 'Let me go!' screamed the man. His face was white, and his eyes were rolling wildly. He was sweating with fear. He still held his rifle. 'Let me go!' he screamed again.

'Why — What?' Henry
tried to ask his question.
'Well, then!' shouted the man with
wild anger. He swung his rifle. It
crashed down on Henry's head.

The fight against pain

Henry let go. All the strength left his muscles. He saw
blinding flashes of light before his eyes. Thunder roared
inside his head. Suddenly his legs seemed to die. He
10 sank to the ground. He tried to rise and fight against
the terrible pain, but it was a hard struggle. Sometimes
he managed to sit up, but he fell down again at once.
His face was grey and covered with cold sweat. Deep
cries of pain were torn from his body.

15 At last, with a twisting movement, he got up on his
hands and knees. From there, like a baby learning to
walk, he got up on his feet. Pressing his hands to his
head, he staggered over the grass.

He struggled with his sick body. His dull senses
20 wanted him to collapse and faint, but he fought against
them. His mind imagined the things that could happen
to a man who fainted in that terrible place. He imagined
quiet places where he could fall and lie in peace. In
his search for a place like this, he swam against the tide
25 of his pain.

Once, he put his hand to the top of his head and touched the wound. The pain forced a cry through his tightly-shut teeth. His fingers were covered with blood. He looked at them stupidly.

Into the darkness

Around him, he could hear the wheels of the big guns moving as the sweating horses were whipped along. Once, a young officer on a tired horse nearly rode over him. The blue light of evening fell across the field. The lines of trees in the woods threw long purple shadows over the grass. The western sky was blood-red.

As Henry left the scene, he suddenly heard the big guns roar. He imagined them shaking with black anger. They roared and spat like iron devils guarding a gate. The air was filled with their thunder and the crash of rifle-fire. Henry turned to look behind him. He saw sheets of orange light in the dark distance. At times, he saw brighter flashes of light, and dark groups of men moving about.

He hurried on into the darkness. The daylight faded until he could hardly see his own feet. But he could hear the noise of shouting, arguing men. Sometimes he could see their dark shapes moving against the dark blue sky. A great crowd of men and supplies spread all around him, in the woods and over the fields.

The road was empty now. Here and there a wagon lay on its side like a dead beast. The bodies of horses and the broken parts of war machines lay everywhere.

The pain of his wound was less sharp now. Henry kept his head very still, and walked very carefully. His face was pale and anxious. His thoughts, as he walked, were fixed upon his wound. There was a cool, wet feeling about it. He imagined the blood moving slowly

down through his hair. His head felt swollen and heavy
on his tired neck. Then he realized his head was not
hurting any more. This frightened him. He imagined
terrible things happening inside his brain.

A kind man

Presently, he felt a heavy tiredness. His head hung
forward and his shoulders were bent as if he carried a
great bundle. He dragged his tired feet along the
ground. He did not know what to do. Sometimes he
wanted to lie down and go to sleep at once. Then he
decided to drag himself a little further.

Someone spoke to him: 'Hullo, son. What's the matter
with you? Are you in trouble?'

Henry nodded. 'Uh!' he agreed. The owner of the
voice took him firmly by the arm. 'Well,' he said with
a friendly laugh, 'I'm going your way. The whole army
is going your way. And I expect I can help you along.'
He supported Henry against his strong shoulder.

As they walked along, the man questioned Henry
gently. He helped him with the replies like a kind
teacher in school. Sometimes he added little stories of
his own. 'What regiment are you with, son? What's that?
The 304th, you say? Why, what brigade is that in? Oh,
is it? I thought they weren't fighting today — they're
right over there, in the centre … Oh, they were fighting,
were they? Well, nearly everybody got their share of
fighting today. My God, I thought I was going to die.
There was shooting all over the place, in the darkness.
And now these woods are a terrible mess. I'll be
surprised if we find our regiments tonight … But soon
we'll start meeting guards, and I expect they'll tell us
exactly where to go. How did you get into these woods,
anyway? Your regiment is a long way from here, isn't
it? Well, I expect we can find it.'

Henry is saved

In the search that followed, the man did everything to help Henry. He found a way for them through the dark forest and guided them neatly over the difficult ground. Henry followed him blindly. At last the man said, 'Ah, there you are, son! Do you see that fire?'

Henry nodded stupidly.

'Well, that's where your regiment is, son. And now, goodbye, and good luck to you.' A warm, strong hand seized Henry's cold, weak one for a moment. Then he was gone. Henry heard the man whistling boldly and merrily as he marched away. As his new friend disappeared into the darkness, Henry suddenly realized that he had never seen the man's face.

Henry moved slowly towards the bright fire. As he staggered forwards, he wondered what kind of welcome his companions would give him. He had to invent a good story to explain his absence, but his tired brain refused to help.

He staggered towards the fire. He could see the shapes of men, throwing black shadows in the red light. As he went nearer, he realized that many more men were asleep on the ground.

Suddenly, he saw a huge black shape in front of him. A gun shone in the firelight. 'Who goes there?' said a fierce voice. For a moment, Henry was afraid. Then he thought he recognized the voice. He called out, 'Why, hello — is that you, Wilson?'

The loud soldier came slowly forward. He stared into Henry's face. 'Why, Henry Fleming — is that you, Henry?'

'Yes — it's, it's me.'

'Well, well, old boy,' said Wilson. 'My word, I'm glad to see you! We thought you were dead.'

Henry tells his story

Henry found that he could hardly stand. His heart sank
and his knees felt like rubber. Now, he thought, now,
I must think of a good story, to protect myself. So,
5   staggering before the loud soldier, he began weakly:
'Yes, yes — I've had an awful time. I've been all over
the place. Right over there, on the right. Terrible fighting
over there — I had an awful time … I got separated
from the regiment … Over there on the right — I got
10 shot. In the head.'

His friend stepped forward. 'What? Shot, you say?
Why didn't you say that at first? I'll call the corporal.'

Another dark shape appeared. It was the corporal
himself. 'Who are you talking to, Wilson? You're not
15 much use as a guard! Why, hello, Henry, is that you? I
thought you were dead! Thank God, our men just keep
coming back! We thought we'd lost forty-two. But if
they keep coming back like this, we'll all be together
again by morning … Where were you?'

20 'Over there on the right. I got separated, and I got
shot in the head —' Henry began again. He was getting
quite good at telling his new story.

Kind Wilson

The corporal led Henry forward. 'Come on over here,
25 son, I'll take care of you. Get back on guard, Wilson.
I'll send someone to relieve you in a minute.'

As the corporal helped Henry along, Wilson called
out after them: 'Put him to sleep in my blanket. And —
wait a minute — here's my water-bottle. There's coffee
30 in it. Look at his head by the fire and see how bad it
is. When they relieve me in a few minutes, I'll come
and look after him.'

Henry was so sick and faint with tiredness that his friend's voice sounded very far away. He could hardly feel the corporal's hand on his arm. He let the corporal guide him.

The corporal led him into the light of the fire. 'Now, Henry,' he said, 'let me have a look at your head.' 5

Henry sat down obediently. The corporal put down his gun and began to feel gently among Henry's hair. He pulled back his lips and whistled through his teeth when his fingers found the lump. 10

'Ah, here we are!' he said. He felt again, very gently. 'Just as I thought. A bullet just brushed you, Henry. It's made a big lump. Just like a bang on the head with a stick. It stopped bleeding a long time ago, but you'll have an awful headache in the morning, Henry. And 15 maybe your mouth will feel dry. You might feel a bit sick, too. But I don't think you're badly hurt. You've been lucky, old boy.' 20

8

A MAN OF EXPERIENCE

Looking around

The corporal walked away. Henry stayed by the fire,
left there like a forgotten parcel. He stared into the
glowing wood and began to feel sleepy. After a time,
5 he woke up a little and looked around. He saw that
the ground in the deep shadows was covered with
sleeping men in every possible position. On the other
side of the fire, an officer was asleep. He was sitting
up straight with his back against a tree. He had gone
10 to sleep with his sword in his arms. But the weapon
had fallen from his hands, and now it lay on the ground
beside him.

In the red and orange light of the fire, Henry saw
other soldiers sleeping. Some lay like dead men. Others
15 moved anxiously in their sleep. The fire gave a cheerful
glow. Above it, branches moved softly. The leaves
shone silver and red in the firelight. Far away to the
right, through a clear space in the woods, Henry saw
the stars. They were like shining stones in the black
20 pool of the night.

The kind nurse

Wilson came along, carrying two water-bottles. 'Well
now, Henry,' he said, 'we'll soon make you better.' He
was like a busy, kind nurse. He put more sticks on the
25 fire, until the flames burned brightly. He made Henry
drink from the water-bottle that contained coffee. To
Henry it was the most wonderful drink in the world.

The warm liquid ran softly down his swollen throat. When he had finished, he sighed with comfortable delight.

Wilson watched his companion with a satisfied look on his face. Then he produced from his pocket a large handkerchief. He folded it into a kind of bandage and poured water onto it from the other water-bottle. He tied it round Henry's wounded head.

'There,' he said, 'you look awful, but I expect you feel better.'

Henry gave Wilson a grateful look. The cold, wet cloth felt wonderful on his aching, swelling head.

After that, Wilson found Henry some blankets, and helped him settle down for the night. Henry felt a most pleasant tiredness spread through his whole body. The warm comfort of the blanket was all round him. His head fell forward on his arm and his tired eyes closed. He heard the sound of guns in the distance. Do they ever stop? he wondered. Then he found that he did not really care. He gave a deep sigh, pulled his blanket closer round his ears, and fell asleep.

When Henry woke, it seemed to him that he had been asleep for a thousand years. At first he did not know where he was. The grey fog of dawn was slowly clearing in the first golden rays of the sun. A light shone in the eastern sky. The air was cold, and Henry was grateful for his blankets. He stared for a while at the leaves over his head.

Henry could hear fighting in the distance. It seemed to go on and on. Around him lay the rows and groups of sleeping men. He had seen them faintly the night before. Now the cold light of dawn shone on their pale, dirty faces. They lay there in strange, uncomfortable positions, and for a moment, they looked to Henry like dead men. He sat up with a little cry of fear. Then he

realized where he was, and what was going on. The men were not dead yet. But by evening, many of them might be.

A new day

Then he noticed the friendly glow of a camp fire. He turned his head and saw his friend Wilson moving busily about a small blaze. A few other shapes moved in the fog. Henry heard the sound of axes on wood.

Suddenly, there was a rolling sound of drums. A distant bugle sang. Other bugles answered, in other parts of the woods. The bugles called to each other like hunting eagles. Close by, the drums of their regiment rolled and thundered.

The group of men in the woods came to life. Many were cursing softly, complaining about the early start and the cold weather. An officer's sharp voice rang out, and the men moved faster. They rubbed their eyes and got ready for a new day.

Henry sat up and gave a huge yawn. 'Thunder!' he remarked. He rubbed his eyes, then he put up his hand and very carefully felt the bandage over his wound. His friend noticed that he was awake, and came over to see him.

'Why, Henry,' he said, 'how are you feeling this morning? Let me look at your bandage.' He began to undo the bandage, but Henry exploded.

'Leave me alone!' he shouted. 'Take your great, ugly hands away. Why can't you be more gentle?' He looked angrily at his friend.

Wilson answered gently, 'Well, now, come and get some breakfast. Then perhaps you'll feel better.'   5

A wonderful change

By the fire, Wilson got Henry some breakfast with great kindness and care. He cooked some fresh meat on a stick for him. He sat and watched Henry eat. There was a look of deep satisfaction on his face.   10

Henry noticed a wonderful change in his companion, since those days of camp life on the river bank. Wilson did not seem to have any doubts about himself any more. He was sure of himself, and so he did not lose his temper with other people so easily. He was not a   15 loud, young soldier any more. He was quiet and wise and confident. He had learnt to live at peace with other people, and with himself.

What has changed him? thought Henry. When did he learn to trust himself? Where did he get this new   20 confidence? He will be much easier to live with, now!

'Well, Henry,' Wilson said, 'what do you think will happen today? Do you think we'll hammer them?'

Henry thought for a moment. 'The day before yesterday,' he finally replied, 'you were sure you could   25 hammer the whole rebel army all by yourself.'

His friend looked surprised. 'Was I?' he said. He thought for a moment. 'Well, perhaps I was,' he decided at last. He stared into the fire. 'You know, Henry,' he added, 'I was a fool in those days, wasn't I?' He spoke   30 as if it had happened many years before. There was a little silence. 'All the officers say we've got the rebels in a tight corner,' he went on at last. 'They all seem to think we've got the enemy just where we want them.'

'I don't know about that,' Henry replied. 'The things I saw over there on the right made me think it was quite the opposite.' Then a sudden thought came to him. 'Oh, Wilson — Jim Conklin's dead.'

His friend stared. 'What? Is he? Jim Conklin?'

'Yes, he's dead. He was shot in the side.'

'Poor Jim.'

A quarrel

All around them, the other small fires were surrounded by men with their little black pots. A quarrel had started at one fire. Two young soldiers had spilt coffee over a huge corporal. The corporal roared and cursed. A fight looked likely.

Wilson stood up and spoke to them. 'Oh, here, boys,' he said, 'What's the use of fighting now? We'll be fighting the rebels in an hour. Don't let's fight among ourselves.'

One of the young soldiers looked at Wilson with a red, angry face. 'You needn't come around here, peace-making. I know you haven't done much fighting since Charley Morgan beat you! But this is a private fight, and it's none of your business!'

'That's true,' agreed Wilson. 'Still, I hate to see —'

The loud argument continued. The corporal accused the two young ones; they accused him. Somehow, in the argument, they lost the desire to fight.

Wilson returned to his old seat. In a few moments, the other three were talking quietly among themselves. They were friends again.

Henry laughed. 'You've changed a lot, Wilson,' he said. 'You were never like this before.' 5

'That's true,' said his friend with a thoughtful smile.

There was another little silence. 'The regiment lost over half its men yesterday,' said Wilson finally. 'I thought they were all dead, of course. But, my word, they kept coming back in the night. In the end, we 10 realized we'd only lost a few. They just got scattered all over the place. They got lost in the woods, and fought with other regiments ... Just like you, Henry.'

Henry said nothing.

New faith 15

The regiment stood and waited for the command to march. Suddenly, Henry remembered something — the little yellow packet that Wilson had asked him to look after. He turned towards his friend. 'Wilson!'

'What?' 20

His friend was staring thoughtfully down the road. Something in the expression on his face made Henry change his mind. 'Oh, nothing,' he said at last.

His friend looked at him in surprise. 'What were you going to say, Henry?' 25

'Oh, nothing,' repeated Henry. He did not want to hurt his friend's feelings ... He gave it to me at a weak moment, Henry thought. He thought he was going to die. Now he's still alive, and I've still got the packet. Perhaps he feels ashamed about it. Poor lad! 30

Henry himself no longer felt ashamed. No one knew the truth about him, after all. He had made all his mistakes in the dark, so he was still a man. He could hold his head up high again. He remembered his adventures of the day before, and looked at them from a safe distance. They began to seem quite brave and exciting. His pain and fear were forgotten.

5 Henry did not give a great deal of thought to the battles that lay ahead. Let the generals do the thinking, he decided. He had learnt his lesson the day before. It was possible to behave badly without anyone knowing. He had done it once, and he could do it again.

10 A new faith in himself secretly appeared inside Henry. A little flower of confidence was growing. He was an old soldier now, a man of experience. He had been out among the dragons of war, and he had found that they were not so terrible after all. A man could 15 escape them, with luck and a good pair of legs.

He was shaken out of his day-dream by his friend. Wilson suddenly gave an anxious little cough. 'Fleming!' he said. He put his hand up to his mouth and coughed again. 'Well,' he said at last, 'perhaps you'd better give 20 me back those letters.'

His face was red; he avoided Henry's eyes.

'All right, Wilson,' said Henry. He put his hand inside his coat and slowly took out the packet. As he held it out to Wilson, the other man turned away from him.

25 Wilson was very ashamed. Henry saw this, and he himself felt braver and more confident. Poor Wilson, he thought with gentle pity. He feels ashamed about it. Poor lad!

After this, and all his other adventures, Henry felt 30 quite ready and able to return home and tell his story. He was ready to make all their hearts glow with stories of war. He could see himself in a warm room, telling everyone his experiences. He imagined his mother's proud face and the admiring eyes of the girls. These 35 were pleasant thoughts.

9
THE HERO

On the edge of the woods

The crack of rifle shots surrounded them. Later, the
batteries joined the argument too. Henry's regiment
marched to relieve another one. The men took up their
positions behind a line of holes that had been dug along   5
the edge of the woods. Before them was a flat piece of
ground. Its trees had been cut down. From the woods
beyond this area, they could hear the loud noise of the
skirmishers shooting in the fog. From the right came
the thunder of a fiercer battle.   10

The men sheltered in their little holes and sat waiting
for their turn to fight. Henry's friend Wilson lay down,
buried his face in his arms and fell asleep. Henry looked
at the woods and up and down the line of soldiers. He
could see the low line of holes for a short distance,   15
then the trees got in the way. A few flags waved lazily
over the little earth hills
in front of the holes.

Always the noise of skirmishers came from the woods to the front and to the left. The noise on the right grew very loud. The guns roared all the time; they did not even seem to stop for breath. Their thunder drowned out every other sound.

Henry wanted to make a joke — something he had read in the newspapers. He wanted to say 'All quiet on the battlefield'. But the noise of the guns was so loud that he never finished the sentence. Then the guns stopped. In the silence, stories began to fly like birds among the waiting men. They were not cheerful stories, and the men feared the worst.

Complaints

Before the sun had driven the grey fog away, the regiment was marching carefully back through the woods. Sometimes, they could see the untidy lines of the enemy, hurrying through the trees behind them. They were shouting in high, excited voices.

When Henry saw them, he forgot his own worries and became very angry. He exploded in loud sentences. 'My God,' he cried, 'our generals are a bunch of fools!'

'Maybe it's not all their fault,' said Wilson in a tired voice. He was marching along with bent shoulders and a tired, defeated look on his face. 'The generals did their best. It's just their bad luck to get beaten so often.

'Well, we fought like devils, yesterday, didn't we? Didn't we do all we could?' asked Henry loudly. He went on to repeat something he had heard at the camp that morning. 'The brigade commander said he never saw a new regiment fight the way we fought. And I don't suppose we were the only ones. Well, then, you can't say it's the army's fault, can you? If we fight like devils, and we still don't win, it must be the generals' fault,' said Henry angrily.

An old soldier who was marching at his side spoke up. 'Perhaps you think you fought the whole battle yourself yesterday, Henry Fleming,' he remarked.

These words hurt Henry. Deep inside, he trembled with fear. He gave a frightened look at the older man. 'Why, no,' he said quickly, 'I don't think I fought the whole battle.'

He watched the other man's face anxiously. But the old soldier did not know the truth; he just liked his joke. Now he accepted Henry's words with a laugh. Henry, however, felt threatened. He remembered the day before, and he was quiet for a while.

Chased by the dragon

The men talked softly among themselves. Their officers were impatient and sharp. Their faces showed that something was very wrong. The men marched along with tired, unsmiling faces. Once someone laughed. Ten or twelve angry faces immediately turned towards him. He did not laugh again.

The noise of guns followed the marching soldiers. Sometimes, the sound faded, but it always came back to bother them. The men cursed under their breath.

The gunfire increased as the sun rose. It grew to a roar, and the woods were filled with short, sharp cracks and flashes as if the trees were on fire.

'Oh dear,' said a soldier, 'it's all starting again.'

A battery had moved into position behind them and was firing into the distance. The regiment waited for the battle to begin. 'Good God,' said Henry, 'we're always chased around like rats! It makes me sick. Nobody seems to know where we're going or why. They just send us here and send us there, and we get hammered here, and hammered there, and nobody

knows why. It makes me feel like a blind cat in a bag.
Now, I'd like to know why they marched us into these
woods anyway — unless they just wanted to give the
rebels a chance to shoot at us. It's …'

5   Wilson interrupted him with a voice full of calm
confidence.

'It'll be all right in the end,' he said.

'Don't tell me,' Henry said angrily. 'I know —'

Just then the lieutenant interrupted the argument. 'Be
10   quiet, you two! Don't waste your breath arguing. Let's
have less talking and more fighting!'

The winds of battle

The sun shone brightly on the forest. The winds of
battle swept towards the part of the line where Henry's
15   regiment lay. The men waited. It was like the calm
before the storm. Then one rifle flashed from the bushes
in front of the regiment. In a moment it was joined by
many others. A huge song of bangs and crashes rang
out. The big guns behind them answered back with a
20   roar. More big guns joined the argument. The battle roar
became a rolling thunder, which went on and on like
a single, continuing explosion.

In the regiment, there was a strange kind of
hesitation. The men were tired out. They had slept very
25   little after long hours of effort. They looked anxiously
around as they stood and waited for the full force of
the battle to reach them.

The advance of the enemy continued. Henry was
wild with anger and impatience. He looked with hate
30   at the battle smoke that floated towards them. Why can't
they let us rest? he thought. Why can't I have time to
sit down and think?

He wanted time to discuss the war with other experienced men. His body was sore and stiff, too. He wanted to rest. But the rebels never seemed to get tired. They were attacking as eagerly as ever. Henry hated them for it. He leaned over and spoke into Wilson's ear. 'If they go on chasing us, they'd better take care — I can't bear much more of this.'

Wilson replied calmly, 'If they go on chasing us, they'll drive us all into the river.'

Henry gave a savage little cry. His eyes burned with hate, and his teeth were tightly shut. The bandage was still round his head. On it, over his wound, there was a spot of dried blood. His hair hung like rats' tails over the bandage. His coat and shirt were open at the neck, and showed his young brown throat. His fingers held his rifle tightly. He felt like a hunted beast. He longed to fight back.

Henry does his best

The winds of battle again swept all round the regiment — the enemy had finally reached them. A rifle flashed in front. At once it was followed by others, and a moment later, the regiment answered back with a roar. A thick wall of smoke settled slowly down. Shots from the rifles cut and tore through it angrily.

To Henry, the fighters were like wild beasts, fighting against a terrible enemy. He felt that his rifle was useless against their strength. Then he forgot everything except his hate and his desire to wipe the glittering smile of victory from his enemies' faces.

Henry was not conscious that he was up on his feet. Indeed, he once lost his balance and fell, but was up again immediately, fighting like a devil.

He took up his position behind a little tree. He was determined to defend that position against the whole world. He did not expect his army to succeed that day, but he was determined to do his best. The crowd surrounded him. He lost all sense of time and place, except that he knew where the enemy lay.

The hot smoke from the gunfire burned his skin. His rifle grew hot, but he never noticed. He kept on loading bullets into it, aiming and firing. Every time he fired, he gave a little growl of satisfaction. When the enemy fell back a little, he rushed forward. And when he had to give way again, he did so slowly and unwillingly.

Once, in his blind, deaf hate, he was still firing when all the men around him had stopped. He was not conscious of the silence. Then his lieutenant laughed. 'You blind fool,' he called. 'Can't you stop shooting? There isn't anything to shoot at!'

Hot work!

Henry turned then and looked back at his companions. They were all staring at him in surprise. He looked in front of him again and saw a deserted battlefield. For a moment he looked puzzled. Then he realized. 'Sorry,' he said. He returned to his companions and lay down to rest. His body seemed to be on fire, and the noises of battle still rang in his ears. He felt for his water-bottle.

The young lieutenant shouted with delight. He called out to Henry: 'My God, if I had ten thousand wild-cats like you, I could win this war in less than a week!' He looked proudly at Henry, and some of the other men gave him admiring looks.

'Are you all right, Henry?' Wilson asked anxiously. 'There's nothing wrong with you, is there?'

'No,' said Henry with difficulty. His throat was very sore. He thought about the events of the past few minutes. He realized that he had fought like a wild beast. He also realized how easy it had been. I looked pretty brave, he said to himself. I thought it was going to be hard, and it wasn't. It was as simple as breathing. I am this thing that they call a hero — me! Strange … He realized that he had not been conscious of any change in himself. He had been a coward. Now, he was brave … It's like waking up and finding that it's your birthday, thought Henry. Now I'm a hero.

He enjoyed the admiring stares. The lieutenant was enjoying himself too. 'Hot work! Hot work!' he repeated to himself as he marched up and down. He was excited and eager.

The men were pleased with themselves as well. 'By thunder, the army will never see another new regiment like us!'

'You're right!'

'The rebels lost a lot of men. If an old woman swept the woods with her brush, she'd get a pile of them.'

'Yes, and if she comes round again in an hour, she'll get a whole lot more!'

The forest was still filled with the sounds of war. The crash of rifles rolled through the woods. Strange flashes of flame lit up the trees. A cloud of smoke floated up towards the sun. And yet, all the time, the sun shone brightly in the calm blue sky.

REAL ACTION

Looking for water

The tired regiment had a few minutes rest, but during this time, the struggle in the forest grew fiercer. The trees seemed to tremble with gunfire, and the ground
5 shook under the heavy feet of the men. The voices of the batteries went on with their long argument. It was hard to breathe in the thick air. The men longed for a bit of clean air, and their throats burned for water.

One man was shot through the body in the heat of
10 the battle. Now that the battle noises were less terrible, the men could hear his screams. 'Who is it?'

'It's Jimmy Rogers.'

When they first saw him, there was sudden silence. They seemed afraid to go near him. He was rolling
15 about on the grass and twisting his trembling body into many strange positions. He looked at them all with hate, and screamed curses at them.

Wilson thought he knew where to find a stream. At once everyone wanted him to get water for them. 'Here,
20 fill my water-bottle, Wilson.' 'And mine, please.' 'Bring me some too.' He left loaded with bottles, and Henry went with him. Henry wanted to throw his burning body into cold water and bathe while he drank.

But they were disappointed. They did not find any
25 stream. They started back.

They were facing the field of battle now. They had a much better view than from their old positions in the smoke. They looked past their own regiment and saw other regiments moving into position. The sunlight glittered on the bright steel of their weapons. Behind them, Henry and Wilson saw a distant road. It curved over a slope. It was crowded with soldiers leaving the battlefield. From the thick woods rose the smoke and dust of the battle. The air was always full of noise.

Near where they stood, balls from the batteries screamed through the air. Bullets flew past. Wounded men, men who had lost their regiments, and cowards were creeping through the woods.

Farm boys

The two young soldiers looked down between the trees and saw a general and his officers. They almost rode over a wounded man who was crawling along on his hands and knees. The general was a fine rider; he guided his horse safely past the man. The man hurried painfully to get out of the path of the other riders. His strength failed him just as he reached a place of safety. One of his arms gave way suddenly, and he fell over on his back. He lay stretched out, breathing gently.

A moment later, the general and his officers stood in front of Henry and Wilson. Another officer rode up to the general. No one noticed the two young soldiers. They stayed there; they wanted to hear the conversation. Their regiment was always hungry for news.

The general spoke calmly. 'The enemy's getting into position over there, ready for another charge. I'm afraid our line will break unless we fight like devils to stop them.'

The other officer cursed at his horse, which seemed impatient to move off. Then he answered, 'It'll be a hard job to stop them.'

'I expect so,' remarked the general. 'What men can you spare?'

The officer thought
for a moment. 'Well,' he
said, 'there's the 304th.
They fight like a lot of farm
5   boys. I can spare them.'
Henry and his friend looked
at each other in surprise. Farm boys! Their regiment?

The general spoke sharply. 'Get them ready then. I'll
watch from here, and I'll tell you when to start them
10 off.'

As the other officer turned to ride away, the general
called to him in a serious voice: 'I don't believe many
of your farm boys will get back alive.' The other
shouted something in reply. He smiled.

15 With frightened faces, Henry and Wilson hurried back
to the line. These events had happened in a very short
time, but Henry suddenly felt much older because of
them. He saw things in a different light. The most
surprising thing of all was to learn how unimportant he
20 was. The officer had talked about his regiment as a
woman talks about a brush. Some part of the woods
needs sweeping — use the brush, then, and never mind
what happens to it afterwards. It was war, no doubt,
but it seemed strange to Henry.

Getting into position

The two soldiers told their news to the lieutenant. 'We're going to charge — we're going to charge!' shouted Henry.

'Charge?' cried the lieutenant. 'Well, my word — this is a bit of real action at last!' His face looked excited and eager.

A little group of soldiers surrounded Henry and Wilson. 'Are we really? Well!' 'Charge! What for? What at?' 'Wilson, you're telling lies!'

'It's all true,' said Wilson.

'That's right,' agreed Henry. 'We heard them talking.'

They caught sight of two riders a short distance away. One was the colonel of their regiment. The other was the officer who had received orders from the general. Henry pointed towards them. 'There you are,' he said. 'We're getting our orders now.'

Their companions accepted the story now. They settled back into their comfortable positions and thought about the news. It was an interesting thing to think about. Many tightened their belts carefully and pulled up their trousers.

A moment later, the officers began to move among the men, pushing them into position. They were like farmers gathering their sheep together. Presently, the whole regiment seemed to take a deep breath. They were ready. Many pairs of glittering eyes stared from the dirty, sweating faces, towards the deeper woods.

The noises of battle surrounded them. The rest of the army was busy with its own quarrel. The regiment had to settle this small argument alone.

Henry turned and gave Wilson a questioning look. Wilson looked back at him. They were the only ones who knew what was really going on. "Farm boys —

don't believe many will get back alive ... " It was their
secret. Still, they read no hesitation in each other's faces.
They nodded in silent agreement when a man near
them said in a quiet voice, 'They'll swallow us, that's
what they'll do.'

The charge

Henry looked ahead. Terrible things seemed to be
hiding among the leaves. The order to charge came.
The messenger was an eager young lieutenant. With a
faint cheer, the regiment began its run. Henry ran with
the rest of them. He aimed for a distant group of trees.
He ran forwards at top speed. His face was hard and
tight. With his torn uniform and his bandage with the
spot of blood on it, he was a strange, wild creature.

The regiment moved from its old position, out to a
clear space in the wood. In front of it, shots rang out
and yellow flames leapt forward. Henry was running at
the front of the line. His eyes were still fixed on the
same group of trees. From all around him, the shouts
of the enemy could be heard. The little flames of rifles
leapt from the trees. The song of the bullets was in the
air. Balls from the big guns growled among the tree
tops. One fell right into the middle of a group of men
and exploded in a burst of red fire. Other men were
hit by bullets and fell to the ground in strange, twisted
positions.

The air was clearer now, and it seemed to Henry that
he could see everything in perfect detail. Every blade
of grass was bold and clear. He saw every line in the
dirty, sweating faces of his companions. His mind
photographed everything like a camera. Afterwards, it
was all sharp and clear in his mind, except the question
of why he himself was there.

Growing tired

The men charged forward, cheering wildly. They were blind and deaf to the danger ahead. But presently they grew tired. As if at a signal, the leaders began to slow down a little. Most of their strength and their breath   5
had gone; they moved more carefully now. They had become ordinary men again.

Henry felt that he had run for miles and was now in some unknown land. The moment his regiment stopped advancing, the noise of rifle-fire became a steady roar.   10
Long curtains of smoke spread out before them. Long tongues of yellow flame leapt from the top of a small hill, and bullets whistled through the air.

Now that they were moving more slowly, the men had a chance to see some of their dead and wounded   15
companions. And now the men stood for a moment with their guns loose in their hands, and watched their numbers growing smaller. They stared like a frightened rabbit watching a snake. A strange silence surrounded them.   20

Then, above the roar of the battle came the voice of
the young lieutenant. His face was dark with anger.
'Come on, you fools!' he shouted. 'Come on! You can't
stay here. You must come on.' He said more, but then
his voice was lost in the roar of the guns. 'Come on!'
he shouted, and ran ahead. His men stared at him
stupidly, like sheep. He had to stop and go back for
them. He stood there, with his back to the enemy, and
cursed his men. His whole body trembled with anger.

The advance

Wilson woke from his dream. He rushed forward, then
fell to his knees. He fired an angry shot in the direction
of the enemy. This action woke the men. They were
no longer like sheep. They suddenly remembered their
weapons, and at once began firing. Their officers urged
them forward, and they advanced, firing as they went.
The regiment was like a wagon stuck in the mud. It
moved at last, with many stops and starts. The men
stopped every few steps, to fire and load. In this way,
they moved slowly forwards through the trees.

The shots from the enemy grew fiercer as they
advanced. At last, the thin leaping tongues of flame
seemed to bar their way ahead. The smoke clouds made
it difficult for the regiment to see. Henry, as he passed
through each grey smoke cloud, wondered what lay on
the other side.

The regiment moved painfully forward until there
was an open space between them and the enemy. Here
the men stopped, like men on the sea-shore when the
tide is coming in. They looked puzzled. They did not
know why they had been driven here, or why people
were shooting at them. And they did not know what
to do next.

THE BROKEN-DOWN MACHINE

A mysterious love

As the men stood and stared, the young lieutenant began to shout and curse at them again. He seized Henry by the arm. 'Come on, you fool!' he roared. 'Come on! We'll all get killed if we stay here! We've only got to get across there —' he pointed, '— and then we can —' The rest was lost in a stream of curses. 5

Henry followed the pointing arm. 'Across there?' he repeated doubtfully.

'Certainly. Just across there! We can't stay here,' screamed the lieutenant. He waved his bandaged hand. 'Come on!' He tried to drag Henry along with him. 10

Henry felt a sudden fierce anger against his officer. He pulled himself away. 'You come on, then!' he shouted, '— if you dare!' 15

Together Henry and the lieutenant charged towards the enemy. Wilson rushed after them. The three men began to shout at the man holding the regiment's flag: 'Come on! Come on!' They danced and waved like mad men. The man in charge of the flag swept towards them and started running ahead. The others hesitated for a moment. Then, with a long, sad cry, the torn regiment moved forward and began its new journey. 20

Over the field they went. They were just a few men, thrown like mud at the faces of the enemy. Yellow tongues of flame leapt towards them. A huge cloud of blue smoke hung before them. The thunder of the guns followed close behind. 25

Henry ran like a mad thing to reach the woods before a bullet could reach him. As he ran, a mysterious love grew inside him. He loved the flag of his regiment. It was a beautiful thing. It was a goddess that called him to follow. It was a woman, red and white, hating and loving, that called to him with the voice of his hopes. He felt safer beside it.

Then, in the mad rush, the soldier who carried the flag suddenly fell to the ground. He had been shot. Henry leapt towards the flag and seized it. At the same time, his friend seized it from the other side. Together they tore it out of the dead man's hands and held it up proudly.

The flag

When the two boys turned round with the flag in their hands, they saw that most of their companions had disappeared. The rest of the regiment was staggering back. The men had thrown themselves at the enemy with all their strength, and now, all that strength was gone. They were retreating slowly, with their faces still turned towards the rebel army. Their hot rifles still answered the enemy's shots. Several officers were still screaming orders at the tops of their voices.

'Where the devil are you going?' the young lieutenant asked. A captain with a red beard roared, 'Shoot into them! Shoot into them, you fools!'

Henry and his friend had a small argument over the flag.

'Give it to me!' 'No, let me keep it!' Each felt quite satisfied for the other to have it. But each felt the need to offer to carry the flag, to show his willingness to put himself in danger again. At last, Henry pushed Wilson away and kept the flag.

The regiment — what remained of it — retreated behind a line of trees. There it stopped for a moment to fire at some dark shapes that had begun to follow it. Presently it began its retreat again. By the time the few remaining men had again reached the first open space, they were receiving a terrible rain of bullets.

Most of the men felt tired and discouraged. They accepted the storm of bullets with bent, defeated heads. It was no use fighting them. They felt anger against their officers for sending them out to do the impossible.

However, at the back of the regiment, a few men continued to shoot at the advancing enemy. They seemed determined to cause the enemy as much trouble as possible. The young lieutenant was perhaps the last man in this untidy crowd. His back was towards the enemy. He had been shot in the arm. It hung straight and stiff. Sometimes he forgot about it, and tried to signal to his men with it. Then the pain made him curse angrily.

A march of shame

Henry kept looking behind him. His face wore an angry look. He was thinking about the general who had called them "farm boys". He had thought, we'll show him! But his dreams had flown away when the "farm boys" had hesitated, then retreated. And now the retreat of those farm boys was a march of shame to him.

He still hated the enemy, but he felt a stronger hate for that general. He had called them all farm boys — and been right about it. That was what hurt most of all. He hid his shame and held the flag high, and he encouraged his companions to greater efforts. Between Henry and the angry young lieutenant, a strange friendship grew. Together they drove everyone to try harder, and Wilson did his best to help them.

But the regiment was like a broken-down machine. It had no more power. Those soldiers who were still able to go on were discouraged by the knowledge that others were slipping away to save their own lives. It was hard to think of glory when others were thinking of safety.

A fierce attack

The smoke clouds and flames were as bad as ever. Once Henry looked through a sudden break in a cloud, and saw a crowd of enemy soldiers. To his anxious eyes there seemed to be thousands of them. Their flag flashed before his eyes.

Immediately, as if the lifting of the smoke was a signal, the rebel soldiers gave a shout. A hundred rifle bullets flew towards the retreating regiment. Smoke clouds rolled by as the tired regiment fired back bravely. Henry was deaf from the shouting and the rifle shots.

The retreat seemed to go on for ever. In the clouds of smoke, men seemed to lose their sense of direction. They thought their regiment had lost its way and was marching into danger again. Once, the men at the head of the retreating crowd turned and came pushing back   5
against their companions.

'They're firing at us!' they screamed, and pointed in the direction of their own army's lines. At this cry, a mad fear filled the men. One soldier, who until then had behaved most calmly and bravely, sank down and   10
buried his face in his arms. Another man cursed the general at the top of his voice. Men ran about looking for a way out of all this. And still the bullets flew.

Henry walked boldly into the frightened crowd. He held the flag high. 'Well, Henry,' said Wilson beside   15
him, 'I suppose this is goodbye, old friend.'

'Oh, be quiet, you fool!' replied Henry. He would not look into his friend's eyes.

Here they come!

Henry saw with surprise that the young lieutenant was   20
standing silently, leaning on his sword as an old man leans on a stick. What's happened to his voice? he wondered. There was something very strange about the young lieutenant's silence. He was staring towards the enemy, like a child staring at a distant toy. He was   25
whispering softly to himself.

The men waited for the thick smoke to clear. Then suddenly, the lieutenant found his voice again. 'Here they come, by God!' he shouted. The rest of his words were lost in a roar of wicked thunder from the men's   30
rifles. As the smoke cleared, Henry saw a group of enemy soldiers. They were so near that he could see their faces and the details of their uniforms.

The enemy had been advancing carefully, with their rifles ready for action. But the lieutenant had spotted them. Now their movement had been interrupted by shots from the blue regiment. The rebels had not realized how near their enemies were, or had mistaken their direction. Almost at once, they were lost again in the smoke from the rifles of Henry's companions.

Henry looked around and tried to get a better view of the enemy. There seemed to be a lot of them, and they were firing well. They seemed to be advancing towards the blue regiment, step by step. Henry sat down sadly on the ground with his flag between his knees. Around him, his companions were fighting like wolves. Well, the boys are dying bravely, he thought with satisfaction.

The fight is over

The blows of the enemy grew weaker. Fewer bullets tore the air. Finally, the men stopped firing and looked around to see what was happening. They saw only dark clouds of smoke. No answering shots rang out. The regiment stood still and stared. Presently, the dark smoke rolled away and they saw — nothing. Nothing moved on the ground in front of them. But it was not an empty stage. Many bodies lay on the grass.

When they saw this, many of the men in blue danced with joy. A cheer of delight broke from their dry lips. They had been attacked, and they had fought back and won. They were confident once more. They looked proudly about them, with their smoking rifles in their hands. They were men.

No one threatened them now. They saw the blue lines of their friends a short distance away. A long way off, the noises of battle continued, but their part of the battlefield was suddenly still. They realized they were free. The few remaining men gave a sigh of relief. They gathered themselves together for the retreat.

In this last, short journey, they began to behave strangely. Some, who had been calm and brave in the darkest moments of the fight, were now the most frightened of all. Perhaps they were afraid of being killed in some small, unimportant way, after the time for a real military death was past. Perhaps, too, they were afraid of being killed just before they reached safety. With anxious looks behind them, they hurried back to their own lines. As they reached them, a regiment of old brown soldiers greeted them.

'Where have you been?' 'Why are you coming back?' 'Why didn't you stay there?' 'Was it hot out there, boys?'

There was no reply from the tired, torn regiment. Henry was hurt by the old soldiers' remarks. He wish he could fight them all. The excitement of battle had left him, and he felt tired and sad now. Beside him, the young lieutenant was still cursing softly.

When they arrived at their old position, they saw the ground over which they had just charged. Henry was surprised to see what a short distance it was. At the time it had seemed like miles. He realized, too, that everything had taken a very short time. So much had been crowded into a very small time and space.

12

VICTORY!

Useless donkeys

Henry's companions drank from their water-bottles. They wiped their swollen, sweating faces with bunches of grass.

Henry thought about his own experiences during the charge. Now he had time to be pleased with himself. He felt a deep satisfaction with his part in the fight.

As the regiment rested from its efforts, the general who had called them farm boys rode up to them. He had lost his cap, and his face was dark with anger. He stopped before the colonel of the regiment. 'My God!' he exploded, 'what a mess you made of that!' He tried to speak quietly, but he was too angry, and the soldiers heard every word. 'Good God, man, why did you stop? What a lot of useless donkeys you've got there.'

'We did our best, sir,' said the colonel. 'We went as far as we could.'

'Did you? My God, you didn't get very far! Your job was to keep the enemy busy while Whiterside's brigade attacked on the other side. You didn't succeed, did you? Listen to the guns over there!' He rode away. The men realized what the noises in the distance meant.

The young lieutenant with the wounded arm had heard everything. Now he spoke up bravely. 'I don't care what he says. My boys put up a good fight out there, and anyone who says they didn't is a fool!'

His colonel ordered him to be quiet. The young lieutenant obeyed. But he had said his piece, and he looked pleased with himself. Meanwhile, the news that the regiment had been blamed instead of praised went along the line. The men were hurt and angry. Wilson said, 'What does that general want? Does he think we went out there and played marbles?'

'Oh well,' said Henry, 'I don't suppose he saw much, in all that smoke. He doesn't know what it was like out there.'

'I'm sure you're right,' replied Wilson. 'It's just our bad luck again. There's no fun in fighting for people who don't even thank you afterwards. Perhaps I'll stay behind next time and let him do it all by himself!'

'Well,' said Henry gently, 'we both did well, and I'll fight any man who says we didn't.'

The two heroes

Just then a group of men hurried towards them. 'Hi, boys, have you heard the news?' they shouted. 'The colonel was talking to your lieutenant. "Young man," he said, "who was that lad who carried the flag?" And our lieutenant answered, "That's Fleming, and he's a real hero." Yes, he did — really he did. "Well," said the colonel, "he is indeed a very brave man. He held the flag up high — I saw him." "You're right," said our lieutenant, "he and a lad called Wilson led the charge, shouting like wild Indians." There, you two, you can put that in your next letter to your mothers. "Well," said the colonel, "they deserve to be generals."'

Henry and Wilson laughed. 'Oh, don't tell stories!' But they exchanged a secret look of joy and satisfaction. They quickly forgot many things. The past held no pictures of shame or disappointment. They were happy, and their hearts swelled with grateful love for the colonel of the regiment and their own lieutenant.

The second charge

The next time they were called upon to charge, Henry
felt calm and confident. As he waited for the order,
Henry watched the battle in the distance. The soldiers
5   marched and fought and fell, and their flags flew like
bright butterflies above them.

When the order came, the tiny regiment charged as
fiercely as ever. With their black faces and wild eyes,
the soldiers looked more like devils than men. The
10 lieutenant led them again. He was still cursing. Henry
wondered how he managed to remember so many
curses, in the heat of battle.

Henry was still carrying the flag, but he did not feel
out of the battle. He was an interested audience, and
15 found the crash and swing of the battle very exciting.
He forgot his tiredness.

A powerful line of rebels came within shooting
distance. The little regiment fired savagely at them. No
order had been given; the men had seen the danger,
20 and fired without waiting for a command. The enemy
soon retreated behind an old fence. From there they
began to fire at the blue men.

They gathered their strength for the struggle. The
general had called them farm boys, then donkeys. They
25 were determined to show him how wrong he was. They
fought like wolves.

Henry decided not to move. I'll just stand here with
the flag, he thought. And if I am killed, he will see me,
and be sorry.

30 Many men were killed and wounded. A corporal was
shot through the cheeks. His mouth hung open,
showing a mess of blood and teeth. He struggled to cry
out. He seemed to think that one good shout would
make him well again

Others fell down at
their companions' feet.
Some of the wounded
crawled away. But
many lay still, with
their bodies twisted
into impossible shapes.

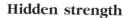

Hidden strength

Henry looked round for his
friend. He saw a fierce, young
stranger and realized it was
Wilson. The lieutenant, too,
was still there, and still cursing
loudly. But the regiment was growing tired again.

The colonel came riding along behind the line. 'We
must charge them!' he shouted. Henry studied the
distance between him and the enemy behind the fence.
He realized they must go forward. Anything else meant
death. He expected his tired, discouraged companions
to be unwilling to attack. But they fixed the sharp steel
blades to their rifles and leapt forward eagerly. They
had found some mysterious, hidden strength. They
charged at top speed, as if they had to get there before
that strength left them for ever. It was a blind and
hopeless charge into the rain of rebel bullets.

Henry kept the bright flag in front and shouted
encouragement. But the men needed no encouraging.
Henry himself felt like the priest of some savage
religion. He felt willing to lay down his life now. Deep
inside he felt a little flash of joy, to find himself so brave.
He ran with all his strength, towards the old wooden
fence where the enemy hid. They won't know what hit
them, he said to himself.

But when he got there, he realized that many of the
rebels were running away. More and more began to
run. As they retreated, a few brave ones stopped to
fire their rifles at the attacking regiment. Only one
5 determined group stayed to fight. They were settled
firmly behind that fence. A flag waved fiercely over
them, as they busily fired their rifles.

The rebel flag

The charging men were very close now. Still the little
10 rebel group stayed and fired. The men in blue threw
themselves at the rebels in a terrible struggle.
Henry's eyes were fixed on the other flag. He was
determined to seize it if he could. He leapt towards it.
His own flag seemed to fly towards it. It was like
15 watching two eagles fighting in the air. Meanwhile, the
regiment was tearing the rebels to pieces.
Suddenly, a bullet hit the soldier in charge of the
rebel flag. He staggered and fell. Still he held onto his
flag. Then Wilson leapt forward and seized the flag. He
20 held it up with a wild cry of victory. His companions
cheered and threw their caps in the air. Victory!
The men in blue sat down on the opposite site of
the fence and rested in the long grass. Henry rested his
flag against the fence, but Wilson would not let go of
25 his new treasure. He held the flag tightly to his chest.

The past

The roar of the battle faded away. Henry and Wilson
could hardly believe it. The thunder of the guns had
been a part of life for so long. They looked around
30 them. Men and guns moved about on the battlefield,
but there was no fighting going on.

They waited for orders. Soon,
the regiment was told to go back to
its old position. The men got up stiffly
and marched slowly back over the battlefield. Not
long before, they had charged across it at top speed. 5

They joined the rest of the army and marched
towards the river. Henry breathed a sigh of relief. 'Well,
it's over,' he said.

Wilson looked around. 'You're right,' he said, 'it is.'

Henry found it hard to think clearly. The battle was over. He had travelled through a mad, savage world and had come out alive. At first, he felt only relief.

Then he began to study his actions: the failures and the successes. They flashed before his eyes, and his brave deeds shone red and gold. He saw that he was indeed "a real hero", as the officer had said.

Then the ghost of his earlier retreat appeared, and his face went hot and red with shame. He remembered the soldier who had been with him when Jim died, too. He remembered that he had treated the wounded man cruelly. 'Oh, God!' he cried aloud.

'What's the matter, Henry?' asked Wilson. But Henry could not answer.

A man at last

As he marched along among his cheerful companions, the memory of his cruelty hung over him and made the red and gold deeds seem poor and cheap. At last he pushed it away, and was able to look at it from a safe distance. He found also that he could look calmly at his old doubts and fears. He saw how stupid he had been then. He knew now that he was brave. He no longer needed to prove it, to himself or to anyone else.

And so, as he marched from that place of blood and death, Henry knew he was a man at last — he looked confidently towards a brave, bright future.

It rained. They marched through a sea of mud under a grey sky. Yet Henry smiled. To him the world was beautiful. His terrible experiences faded away like dreams. He forgot the heat, the blood and the sweat of war. He turned eagerly to thoughts of calm blue skies, fresh fields and cool streams. Over the river a golden ray of sun shone through the dark rain clouds.

QUESTIONS AND ACTIVITIES

CHAPTER 1

Which of these things did Henry's mother not say to him when he left home to go to war? What is wrong with the ones she did not say?

1 'I know you can beat the whole rebel army by yourself.'

2 'I've packed a home-made cake for you.'

3 'I want you to be as warm and comfortable as anyone in the army.'

4 'When you get holes in your clothes, just throw them away.'

5 'Never do anything that you'd be ashamed to tell me about.'

6 'Do your duty and always think about me.'

7 'You'll have to keep quiet and do as they tell you.'

CHAPTER 2

Fill in the gaps to say what this part of the story is about. Choose from: **conversation, huge, glittered, uniforms, marching, lighter, regiment, camp, orders, colonel, rider.**

A few days later they woke up very early. In the darkness before dawn, their (1) _____ glowed purple. From across the river, the fires still (2) _____ in the rebel (3) _____. The eastern sky was beginning to get (4) _____. The regiment stood and waited. At last Henry heard the sound of a horse's feet: (5) _____, he thought. A (6) _____ stopped in front of the (7) _____. The two held a short (8) _____. A moment later the regiment began to move off like a (9) _____ animal with many feet. Another dark (10) _____ moved in front of them, and from all around them came the sound of many (11) _____ men.

CHAPTER 3

Choose the right words to say what this part of the story is about.

Henry put up his (1) **hands/rifle** and (2) **fired/found** his first
bullet. The weapon was (3) **loaded/full**. At once Henry was
shooting like a (4) **motor/machine**. He (5) **stopped/started**
worrying about himself. He was not a (6) **child/man** any more.
He was a (7) **wheel/member** of his regiment. All the time he
was (8) **afraid/conscious** of his companions. They were
(9) **brothers/soldiers** in (10) **war/battle**, among the smoke
and the (11) **fear/danger** of death.

CHAPTER 4

*Put the letters of these words in the right order. The first one
is 'terrible'.*

Suddenly the still air was torn by a (1) **rebritle** noise. Surely,
worlds were being torn (2) **tarap**. There were big and small
guns, shouts and (3) **crasems**. Henry (4) **aideming** the two
armies (5) **granite** at each other's (6) **shottar** like mad dogs. He
now (7) **trondoused** that the fight in which he had taken part
was quite small and (8) **toptruminna**. This battle was
(9) **fretfined**. Its noise was huge and earth-(10) **skanigh**.

CHAPTER 5

Put the words at the end of these sentences in the right order.

1	A wounded man …	[at] [marched] [side] [Henry's] [quietly].
2	Henry saw that …	[had] [the] [wounds] [two] [soldier].
3	The wounded man needed …	[friend] [to] [to] [a] [talk].
4	He said that they …	[had] [tigers] [fought] [all] [like].
5	His kind face shone with …	[his] [army] [for] [the] [love].
6	He turned and asked …	[was] [hurt] [Henry] [he] [where].
7	Henry felt ashamed and …	[through] [slid] [crowd] [the] [away].

CHAPTER 6

Find the nine errors in this paragraph.

Henry felt he was watching a regiment of gods and devils, with weapons of flame and flags of fire. I could never be like them, he thought. He was near to fainting. How can they hurry like that? What makes them so quick? As he watched, he did not want to be one of those soldiers marching into battle. In his mind's eye he saw himself leading the attack with a broken gun in his hand and a frightened look on his face. He saw himself dying a coward's death on a horse before the eyes of everyone.

CHAPTER 7

Who said these words? Choose from: **Henry, the corporal, the kind man,** *or* **Wilson.** *You must use some names more than once.*

1 'I got separated from the regiment.'
2 'The whole army is going your way.'
3 'Look at his head by the fire and see how bad it is.'
4 'I'll be surprised if we find our regiments tonight.'
5 'You'll have an awful headache in the morning.'
6 'I'm glad to see you! We thought you were dead.'
7 'I've been all over the place.'
8 'My God, I thought I was going to die.'
9 'I got shot. In the head.'
10 'You've been lucky, old boy.'

CHAPTER 8

What happened when Henry woke up? Choose from sentence (a) or sentence (b).

1 (a) Henry felt as if had been asleep for a few minutes.
   (b) Henry felt as if had been asleep for a thousand years.
2 (a) At first he did not know where he was.
   (b) He immediately remembered where he was.
3 (a) The grey fog was clearing in the first rays of the sun.
   (b) Grey fog gave everything a sense of gloomy sadness.

4 (a) The air was warm, and Henry threw off his blankets.

    (b) The air was cold, and Henry was grateful for his blankets.

5 (a) He stared into the fog, looking for Wilson.

    (b) He stared for a while at the leaves over his head.

6 (a) The distance was full of the noise of fighting.

    (b) The guns were silent — there was no noise of fighting.

CHAPTER 9

Put these sentences in the right order to say what this part of the story is about. The first one is done for you.

1 Henry took up his position behind a little tree.

2 The lieutenant laughed and called him a blind fool.

3 Henry realized he had looked pretty brave, and was a hero.

4 The young lieutenant looked at him proudly.

5 He was still firing when all the others had stopped.

6 Wilson asked Henry if he was all right.

7 He kept on loading bullets into his gun and firing it.

8 Henry returned to his companions and lay down to rest.

CHAPTER 10

Put the beginnings of these sentences with the right endings.

1 The general stood …

2 He said the enemy was …

3 An officer said it would be …

4 He said the 304th fought …

5 Henry told the lieutenant …

6 The lieutenant said it would be …

7 The officers began to move …

8 They were like farmers …

(a) among the men.

(b) like a lot of farm boys.

(c) that they were going to charge.

(d) a hard job to stop them.

(e) a bit of real action at last.

(f) gathering their sheep together.

(g) in front of Henry and Wilson.

(h) getting ready for another charge

CHAPTER 11

The (b) sentences in these paragraphs are in the wrong place. Where should they go?

1 (a) The men stood still and stared. (b) <u>They could see the blue lines of their friends a short distance away.</u> (c) Nothing moved in front of them, but many bodies lay on the grass.

2 (a) When they saw this, they cheered with delight. (b) <u>In this last, short journey, they began to behave strangely.</u> (c) They looked around proudly, with their smoking rifles in their hands.

3 (a) No one threatened them now. (b) <u>Presently the dark smoke rolled away.</u> (c) A long way off, the noises of battle continued, but this part of the battlefield was still.

4 (a) They gathered together to complete their retreat. (b) <u>Henry was surprised to see what a short distance it was.</u> (c) Some who had been brave before, were now the most frightened.

5 (a) The men looked back at the ground over which they had just charged. (b) <u>They had fought back, and won.</u> (c) At the time it had seemed like miles.

CHAPTER 12

Choose the right answer to complete each sentence.

1 Henry studied the distance between him and the enemy. He realized they must go forward. If not, he thought (a) they would die; (b) they would be cowards; (c) they would lose the war.

2 He expected his tired, discouraged companions to be unwilling to attack. They (a) turned back and began to retreat; (b) stood still, not knowing what to do; (c) found some hidden strength, and charged.

3 Henry kept the bright flag in front and shouted encouragement. He felt like (a) he could win the whole war on his own; (b) a hero in one of the old stories; (c) the priest of some savage religion.

4 Henry's eyes were fixed on that other flag. He made up his mind to (a) destroy it; (b) take hold of it; (c) throw it down.

Oxford
Progressive
English Readers